FROM THE AUTHOR

Fiction 4-Pack #1 is a four story collection of my works. In addition to the titles on the cover, there are two bonus pieces of fiction. Both appear here for the first time and tie into forthcoming stories.

Hope you enjoy,
Chris

CHRISTOPHER WATSON

4 FICTION -PACK #1

ELSEWHERE
E
P
PUBLISHING

Fiction 4-Pack #1

Published 2013 by Elsewhere Publishing
www.elsewherepublishing.com

Cover art copyright © Elsewhere Publishing
Book and cover design copyright © 2013 Elsewhere Publishing

ISBN-13: 978-1-62538-013-5

Elsewhere Publishing
www.elsewherepublishing.com

Contents:

Extras:

Dedicated to:
> *family and friends*
> *mentors and minions*
> *Kay McGarvey*

CHRISTOPHER WATSON

4 FICTION -PACK #1

Roach's Run

Deep space exploration ramped up. Though governments search the black with top-notch scientist running expensive robots and drones; corporations cornered the market.

Contracting their staff for little more than room, board, and a promised portion of any find, Prism Corp flings ships into the universe.

The frontline - Suicide Squad - explores with little to live for and often expire before their contracts.

FIVE

"I DIDN'T KNOW THEY CAME THAT BIG."

As usual, Jacobs talks to anyone listening and, as usual, no one answers. Scanning the dark, rocky landscape of this miserable fucking planet for the enemy we outran, I roll my adrenal capsule from under my tongue and clack the metal casing against the inside of my teeth. This cave stinks like a frontline latrine. Reflexively, I make sure I'm not laying in anything slick or slimy.

Four strokes and the pill sprays cherry against my palate. I slide the booster back under my tongue to keep it from fully triggering and suck at the flavor shot to activate the crust-flavored micro-crystals. Homemade cherry pie. Or what it probably tastes like to those rich enough for the real deal.

"Did anyone know they came that big?" Jacobs, the only Chi'Gan to join a Suicide Squad, clicks the clip releases on his pulse pistols. Like most of his kind, in action, he's a gangly blur of taut brown skin over lean muscle and sinew. "Roach?"

Used to me replying, he frowns at my silence.

His upper set of hands moves like lighting, switching clips while his lower set catches the empties and clicks them into the four swap spots on his pack. Pure twitch.

"Have you ever seen anything that big?" When we invaded two hundred years ago, they were lanky bastards with stone spears and pinpoint accuracy. Now, they fight with us and have upgraded to our pulse pistols. "I need an expletive."

"Damn," I suggest.

Dixon, my dream girl if it wasn't for the wedding ring she wore on her middle finger to flip off my advances, offered, "Fuck."

"Profanity is the first resort of the limited mind." Dixon and I share a look at Stripe's opinion—always the goddamn church boy. "Expletives are not necessary."

The rocks are still. The pie flavor is gone. I blow air out and sniff my breath to chase the experience. My nose and mouth make empty promises to my equally empty stomach. Pissed, it growls. We have been on restricted rations for three days now. A wild thought comes and I ask, "Think they're poisonous?"

Dixon drops next to me, a second set of eyes. "I don't think they're bio." She's been clacking too.

Her throat works. I wet my lips. "Is that apple?"

She swallows the flavor burst, and her breath is fresh pie goodness. "Yeah."

"Got an extra?"

"Not apple, but I got the others." She pats her elastic wristband. "Full rainbow pack."

"Want to swap?" I eye the grape pill. "All I got is cherry."

"Mouths shut, eyes out, you two." Stripe barks from behind us. We share another brief look before doing as told. "They have to be bio. They bleed."

"Maybe I said the wrong word." Jacobs hums as Chi'Gan usually do when searching for a human word.

Dixon motions. "Movement at two, Roach."

I find what she points out. When not in combat, the rock creature, a lumbering behemoth, is hard to spot against the other rocks because it moves so damned slow. "How tall would you say it is? Twenty? Thirty?"

"I'd bet my ass it's thirty plus."

I nod. "You're on."

The finger.

"Shut it." Stripe takes a knee between us. "How far?"

I light my optics for five seconds to paint it, my energy reserve drops to sixty-one. "Two hundred and ten meters out." I wink at Dixon. "Twenty-five meters tall."

Again, the finger, but this time with a smile.

I do my best not to scan her body as I return to searching. Mister Dixon is one lucky man.

Jacobs' humming stops. "I need an explosive!"

I roll over and look into his small, recessed eye slits. "No way."

His tunnel vision shoots to Dixon.

She covers the slap-top grenades on her waist. "Fuck that."

Stripe asks, "Are you boom-psych approved?"

"Again, fuck that." She shakes her head at Stripe. "I ain't going to let him pray us to kingdom come."

A set of Jacobs' fists land on his hips while the other arms cross. "Can your race hit a target at three hundred meters?"

She pats her thumper. "That's why we have guns, remember?"

Dixon is not going to give up her slap-tops. I roll back, sniffing at her words, and stare around the area where I painted it. Come on. Move, sucker.

"Dixon." Stripe pauses. He must be giving her his *will you please shut up and let me be diplomatic* face. "Jacobs, before we consider the option, we need to know if you are boom-psych approved."

"You humans make sure we Chi'Gan never get approved."

"Because you fucking prims–"

"Dixon!" Stripe tries to shut her up.

It doesn't work. "–will blow your dumbasses up along with any human stupid enough to trust you." I hear her slap her body. "These aren't tickets to some perverse afterlife where you can hump your ancestors."

Still no movement. My stomach churns. "Something's wrong."

Jacobs gives a brief hum. "Should you not be out hunting?"

Dixon pops to her feet, leaving her thumper. Her fists ball. "Is that some kind of wiseass sexist comment, snout-face?"

There's movement—too much movement. I light my optics, grab her ankle, and squeeze the titanium weave.

"Let me go."

"No." I tug. "Look."

She drops down.

Stripe pivots on his knee.

Jacobs leans over me, his Chi'Gan funk-mouth musking the area, killing what remained of Dixon's apple scent and my appetite.

Dixon and Stripe jack into my feed. The extra draw drops my reserve to sixty. Through me, they can see the fifty, one-meter-tall rock creatures rushing our direction.

Chi'Gan vision is better at night. I wonder what else Jacobs sees when he asks, "Can I have an explosive now?

Two

Driving the burrito into my mouth, I smell the seasoned meat, beans, and cheese after I rip a bite away. The lettuce is cold and crisp, and the sour cream helps temper the searing strip steak and molten filling.

Eyes closed, I hold the two-pound delight under my nose. It warms my hands and I inhale deeply. Chewing, I nod as I swallow a portion.

Being first in the Mess, I hear other squaddies bump through the swinging doors. They clack their trays on the shelf to slide the line to see what's what. Benson and his squad move past the salad and vegetables to the main course. They're wearing operation black fatigues and are rightfully treating this as their possible last meal.

Garcia, now lean with a nubby ponytail, leaves his empty tray to beeline at me, going serpentine through small tables and hopping over longer ones. "Roach!"

I call back, "Garcia." Before taking a bite, I stand and chew the steak-heavy meal. We slap hands and bump chest. His titanium weave makes a weird tinking sound when it contacts my orange cotton. "Damn, you're no longer that bald chubster I had to e-vac on his virgin run."

"Nah, check it." He points to his chest. A nickname is stitched over where the Velcro strap once displayed his last name.

"Spider King?" I pretend to buff it. "Solid." I offer him a chair, sit, and cut my burrito in half. "What's the origin?"

He sits, grabs the unbitten portion, and answers, "NE-73."

"The bug-ball?"

"Yup. The Brains picked up something on the scanners we left behind and sent us back." He takes a bite and chews through his update. "Biggest operation I've ever seen." His mouth continues to move—part chewing, part talking, no sound.

The doors thump open as more squaddies, in stand-down blue, pile in and clack their trays on the food shelf. A general hum fills the mess from conversations, but for some reason, Spider King and his chewing remains silent.

His smacks and chomps come back mid-sentence, "...fifty squads and, using the method of extermination I learned from you when you pulled me from that fucking rock..." He bops the top of his hand to drop his other fist and spread his fingers, imitating a wave rolling across the table. "Pop. Boom! More kills than the rest of them, *combined.*" He smiles a proud new parent's smile and rubs his nickname. "Thus, Spider King."

"So, King." Only a blind man wouldn't have seen how the ten squads were all lumped together at the other side of the Mess Hall. I motion my head to them. "What's with the distance? I've cleared bio-iso."

"Shit, man. You know how worry spreads."

"What's worrisome?"

"You." He moves to thump my chest. Everything goes silent when he gets close to my orange jumper. He knocks twice and pulls his hand back to the table. His mouth hadn't stopped moving, and sound returns in the middle of his sentence. "...you've cleared bio. Everyone just thinks your run on QM-4818 has given you *the crazy*."

"We're all crazy." I turn my back to them and focus on the oozing filling. A burrito is a composite food. No matter what you put in a tortilla, as long as you wrap it a certain way, it's technically a burrito.

I frown and keep my mouth from repeating the unprompted definition.

"Yeah, but-" His eyebrows lift and spread. "Not the *real* crazy."

I use a fork to spear three steak chunks. "Fuck 'em." Strings of cheese dangle from the meat to the mass. "They'll see what's what when I'm back in black."

"Nope." He stands and makes a show of fixing my orange collar before pulling me to my feet and grabbing my tray. "They'll see now."

+

Most hate bioorganic isolation because The Brains make us recall every facet of our latest mission, how it made us feel, and how we think any of it relates to the various objects they display for us. Big Blue is an impossibly huge square room that's been painted light blue. Except for a white bed—a cloud in the sky with a pillow which smells of antiseptic—the room is a large waste of space in the Command Ship.

I've never seen one of the scientists and don't believe there are any. Their voices are probably synthesized by computers pulling and feeding information into our files to make sure our sanity is still, more or less, intact.

Laughing at Benson mocking Young, I realize nothing about bio-iso bothers me more than not having lunch with my fellow squaddies.

Young gets up, about to fire back when he stops and everyone goes quiet. Their eyes train over—and several feet beyond—me before falling away to their food or somewhere else on the table.

I turn to see who's fucking up my bonding time.

A brown crew cut with badges on his tactician gray stamps his heel on the mess hall floor. All squads, black and blue, stand and salute him. Stupid academy kids always want to be saluted.

I hold my tongue, turn back to my cold burrito, and take a bite.

"You." Without Benson's eyes dropping to me, I know he's pointing at my back. "I stomped for presentation."

"And just because you whip your dick out doesn't mean I have to give you a hand job." I glance at Spider King, Benson, and Young standing on the other side of the table. Their faces are serious, but their eyes are wet with held-back laughter. "This area is for squad only. So why don't you slide on to the cushy Tactician Lounge and let us get back to lunch."

"I am a stripe."

"Spoken like you still have a stick jammed up your ass." Why would a Tactician want to dip their toe into grunt work? "Still, no such thing. Either you're squad or you're not." I turn to mock him further and notice his gray is cut in style to match our stand-down fatigues.

I rise.

Scrap and Vault each hook one of my arms to keep me from assaulting an officer. Their titanium weave makes the same weird tinkling sound as Spider King's did before.

"See?" He motions to the uniform like he's show-casing one of those useless fucking badges on his chest. "Now slide over. I'm hungry."

A nod to Scrap and Vault, and they let me go. I straighten my top and process his name strap. "Lawrence, is it?"

He glances at it and gives a slow, patronizing nod. "Yes."

"If you're squad, how many kills you got?"

His chin raises and his chest puffs. "Twenty-seven."

"Quite impressive..."

He smiles.

I continue, "-for a first run." I look around the small sea of black and blue. "Any confirmation?"

No one speaks up.

Lawrence offers, "All of them were confirmed by Command."

"I wasn't talking to you!"

He flinches.

I unclench my fists to sweep an open hand toward my fellow squaddies. "Not one of them has seen you kill, while each of us can confirm nearly all of the others' kills." I motion to his gray uniform and decide to hold back my opinion about Tacticians. I'm sure The Brains are going to have me talk about this when I get back, and if I dump on him too much, they might revoke my lunch rights. So, I shake my head instead and start to turn to my food. "Come back when your kill count grows up."

"I am the only person to stripe into Squad." He glares. "Show me some respect."

Before Scrap or Vault can grab me, I spin and close the distance to get right in his fresh young face. "You're fucking Tac!" He flinches again, but to his credit, he holds his ground as I point between his eyes. "You're not a killer. You study what we do and your kind *advises* us on how to do it better."

Dixon comes over, hovering her wedding band hand between us. I start stepping back as she moves her hand closer to me—controlling me, making me restrain myself in a way no other squad member could. "I'm in iso-orange, so I'm able to tell you what they are dying to say."

His eyes search the other squad members for a different opinion; none comes. They narrow and shift back to me.

My mouth continues to flap as she walks me back-wards. "In a week or so, I'll be back in blue or black and will hold my tongue like these soldiers. But until then, Stripe." I thump into the bench and sit. "Fuck off."

He looks around one more time before walking away.

Benson whispers, "It's good to have you back, Roach."

I face my food, fist bump Benson and then the others who extend their hand. "It's good to be back."

Six

I DIVE FURTHER INTO THE CAVE AND, INSTEAD OF MY chest armor protecting me from the hard rock floor, I splat in something slimy and slide to a wall. It reeks like a rancid mix of decomposing bio mass and shit. To beat the smell, I clack my adrenal pill. Getting a mouthful of cherry on the first strike, I curl my tongue around the booster to keep it stable.

Instead of swallowing, I channel the mist back toward my nasal cavity, and homemade cherry pie temporarily overpowers the stench. Dixon's grenade at the mouth of the cave detonates, rocking the area and ringing my ears.

Darkness spreads. My optics light.

Laying over Dixon to protect her, Stripe calls, "Sealed."

She shoves him away.

His mouth forms a playful schoolboy smile as he grabs at her body in a familiar way.

She bats his hands away.

If Dixon chose him over me... my fingers scoop the mess and my fist balls around something solid in my growing jealous rage.

She decks him across the jaw. The blow shakes his brown crew cut and sends him into the wall.

He's no longer smiling, but I am.

"Humans," Jacobs calls and points to a wall. "Can you see?"

Stripe is cradling his jaw and, in the dark, my smile widens. "I can."

Running a finger over his teeth, he turns his face in our direction. "No."

Dixon is moving toward our voices, fumbling. "My jack came out."

I push to stand but slide a bit further into the slime. "Don't move closer, Dixon." Though she can't see, I point from habit. "Some kind of goo starts halfway into the cave." I stay prone, drop the rock, and dig my hand into muck. Rubbing my fingers together, I note the friction impairment. *Friction impairment?*

She stops. "Is that the stench?"

"Yeah." There are black heaps beneath the yellow slime. "And I got some on me."

Jacobs calls our attention again, his upper arm extended to where he wants us to look. "Humans, there's scrawl here with Todd Dixon's name-symbols."

There is a mister Dixon. My relief at knowing she isn't shacking up with Stripe is killed the moment I see her distraught face.

Though she can't see, Dixon moves through the cave, stumbling toward Jacobs. "Guide me in."

"Here." Jacobs speaks as she moves towards him. "Here." He says again as she starts to veer after tripping on a rock. "Here." His four arms reach out for her. Two of his hands take hold of her wrists to direct her fingers to the wall and the other two land on her shoulders.

I get to my knees in the muck as she drops to hers.

She's never been like this.

Before speaking, I focus my protective desire into resolve before I speak. "If he's still kicking, Dixon, we'll find him and bring him home."

She stifles a sob.

My gut tightens at her loss and I want nothing more than to make her pain go away.

Jacobs goes to his knees to comfort her like I want to, but I'm covered in... who knows what.

+

We lost contact with the other three remaining squads days ago. I sure as hell hope to fuck one of them made it back to tell Command to scrub this motherfucking death trap from the search list.

The race that lives on this planet is highly advanced and makes use of large rock-like robots to do their fighting. Fish killed one of the scorpion bastards before he and Sumner were dragged off into a cave.

This rock has ore that makes our sensors bounce to ten. However, these natives have

17

*made it into an alloy that is the heart of their
trade and defense. Lasers work on the scorps,
but impact is the only answer for the bots...
and we've run out of boom.*

*Here's to hoping the Brains in bio-iso
are not able to pry this planet's resources
from any survivors' minds. And if they
do, I sure as shit hope they send the next
squaddies with nothing but booms.*

*Fuck this place,
Todd A. Dixon 2597.10.24*

P.S. Love you Sarah.

+

Except for that last bit, Dixon's husband sounds as hard as they come. I regret not meeting him. At least now I understand why she gave up her Death Blossom tag to be called Dixon. Maybe I have met him. He's been gone for a year, and no one has mentioned his nick.

Jacobs and Dixon stayed in the cave to alert us if the bots outside start making progress in removing the rubble. To keep from continually choking on my stench, Stripe takes point as we explore deeper into the cave. Jacked in, he walks to the right as not to obscure my optics.

Time to pry. "Hey, Stripe."

His hand still occasionally goes to his chin to rub his jaw. "What, Roach?"

I wait until we round the corner and it's clear. "What was Todd's tag?"

"No idea." Switching his slap-top launcher to his other hand, Stripe gives a grunt and wipes his palm on his pant leg. "He was gone before I joined."

I keep my thumper level. If we round a corner to a bot, I'm going to feed it its first, and last, grenade. "Yeah, no shit he was gone." I lower my head a bit, but the stench on my collar brings my chin and pace up a bit before I slow. It's all over me; there's no way to outrun it. "But you're obsessed with Squad. You've must have jacked off to his stats at least once."

He spins to get in my face.

I meet him halfway. "What?"

"Hope Killer." He's staring. Some deep reserve makes his eyes as hard as true squad. "His confirmed kill count was in the five digits. Though Sarah was loyal to him, he was worse than Chi-Gan, treating every woman as a potential lay."

So this is why he is pissed. He can't get with Dixon. "Don't worry, Stripe. I'm sure once your kills get in the triples and you drop that horrible gray, your chance to bed Dixon will increase."

His eyes shine with momentary hope. "You think?"

The kid is too easy. Again, I set him up for a slam, and he walks right into it. My mouth twitches and I fail to hold the straight face. I let go of my thumper.

He goes to turn away at his own pace, but I grab his shoulder and shove him into the wall as I pull my pulse pistol.

A small flash of light and a tenth of the gun's energy percentile indicate I have fired, but a clicking-squeal at the far end of the cave signals I hit the chitin fucker who came around the corner.

Stripe scrambles to get behind me.

It peeks.

I shoot.

It drops, and the cry stops.

Stripe has recovered his breath. "We got to get the others."

I keep an eye on the thing at the end of the hallway. From what I am guessing is its head, Hope Killer was right. They do resemble scorpions. "Why?"

He nudges me to look as he points at the wall I pushed him against.

My eyes follow down his arm to his fingertip. It's next to Todd Dixon's initials, with an arrow pointing further into the cave.

THREE

ENERGIZED AT BEING ABLE TO SAY WHAT ALL OF THE squaddies were thinking, I return to my intermediate quarters. It's a ten-by-ten with the same light blue from Big Blue covering the ceiling to halfway down the wall, where it becomes a light tan before transitioning to deep, enriched-soil brown.

Sky & Earth. The Prism Corp's motto.

The doorframe beeps as I pass through. It announces, to those monitoring, that I made it back within the allotted hour. A light bell sounds near my coffee cup, and the sweet roast of Chi-Gan beans fill my holding area.

I scoop the cup and steal a sip of the hot, robust flavor of home before passing my hand by the access pad to the bathroom. A denying bong sounds; it's in use by adjoining iso-cubes on the other side.

Content with my coffee, I sit at the desk and wait. The only good thing about being in any stage of bio-iso is that the corp serves coffee from your birth planet.

My Place of Origin use to be a nice sucker bet for free booze. Not many humans are born on what they call E-4, but what I, and the native race, call home.

Taking a deep draw, I hum like a Chi'Gan searching for a word. The vibration brings the flavor across my tongue, and I press my Adam's apple to keep the hum in my mouth.

My thumb brushes against something hard under my collar. Swallowing, I set my coffee aside and fish it out.

A data cube?

Why am I staring at my fingertips? They're positioned like I was holding something small. Did I drop it?

I lift my coffee, sip, and hum. Moving to the other side of the room, I scan where I sat.

Nothing.

The bathroom door chimes and slides open without further sound. I shrug, set my cup down, and enter to empty my bladder. Part of me tries to remember what I had in my hand and the other starts to recollect the first day of my previous mission.

+

The coffee spout buzzed a denial before filling my cup with plain hot water. Working on my initial terrain recall on the holodesk in my ten-by-ten, I had lost track of time *and* how many cups I drank. It must have been five since the good stuff stopped flowing.

From memory, the PC-79 veined canyon walls around my landing site rose a hundred meters and were as accurate as I could make them. A very thin fissure ran the length of the chasm, which sensors indicated led to an underground lake rich with PC-53.

The resources meter pinged an eight on the ten-dot meter for iodine and gold. I remember dancing.

Even split four ways, this was the kind of find squaddies dreamt about. My parents' account would blossom, my dad could get high-end bionics for his blasted-off legs, and my siblings could have their choice of schools. Hell, if I eventually have kids and grandkids, all of their accounts would continually uptick as long as this rock produced.

My stomach sloshes.

A smile forms.

I stand and dance again.

Once this tour was over, I wouldn't have to be Suicide any more. They say we don't adjust well back into society. I probably wouldn't give squad up, but now it would be by choice instead of necessity.

Besides the chime, the bathroom door is normally silent; it slides open with a scrap. Dixon stands there, holding it open. Self-conscious, I can't help but wonder how much of my dancing she witnessed.

An analysis of her slides through: she's in operation black, whiskey fumes radiate from her, and tears roll from her bloodshot green eyes.

She stares at me, and I at her.

One long stride and she's on me.

Dixon's armor makes the same tinking sound when our bodies meet.

From reflex, my arms wrap around her. With will, they squeeze. Her warm mouth tastes of spirits, and I become intoxicated with lust.

My heart is racing when I jolt upright from the holo-desk. The chair shoots across the room and slams into the wall before crashing over.

The brown bed is empty and made. I'm alone and aroused in my ten-by-ten. The only scent in the room is faint Chi'Gan coffee. It sits on a warmer. The hint on my lips, despite my deepest want for it to be whiskey, is from the seasoned burrito meat.

"Are you all right, S.S. Roach?" As usual in bio-iso, The Brains' voice comes from every surface as though dialed directly to my location.

I steady my breathing and check the holodesk. The nearly completed terrain from before had regressed to rough walls, taking on the resemblance of canyons on barren land. "I, I, I."

"You fell asleep while building your terrain recall."

No. That couldn't have been a dream. I saw her tears. I felt her suppleness under the titanium mesh. I tasted the Robb Whiskey on her mouth. I smelled the straw-berry juice she spilled on herself during lunch. I heard her sigh when I squeezed her.

"From what you saw, we are anxious to see if we can upgrade QM-4811 to a Near Earth designation."

Testing, I push my cup for a refill. The rich aroma fills the room as my coffee cup is filled to the rim.

"Your squad's sensors detected high concentrations of 53 and 79."

I pass my hand to the bathroom. The door chimes and slides open without a sound. I step in.

The Brains' voice comes from every surface in the bathroom as I dump my coffee.

"Are you all right, S. S. Roach?"

To see if I can make it grind like Dixon did, I rush to the door, but miss catching it. Moving to the spout, I place my cup, and fragrant deep brown Chi'Gan fills it.

"Your heart rate is elevated."

Another swipe, followed by a chime, and I'm in the bathroom dumping fresh coffee in the toilet.

"You read as distressed."

I move more quickly to the door and slap the doorjamb right after the door disappeared into it. Back at the spout, I answer, "Just trying to figure out how many cups I've had."

The spout buzzed a denial and, instead of hot water, it becomes inactive.

"The answer to your question is three and a half."

I remove the cup and place it under the spout again. Another buzz.

"We will not approve such waste, S.S. Roach. You consumed half a cup before falling a sleep. Upon waking, you filled the cup. Poured it out. Refilled and poured out."

My eyes were fixed on the cup and the spout. From the moment I laid eyes on Dixon, I wanted her, but she was married. She had always been married. Regardless,

I had always wanted her and would do anything for her. Could her proximity in the Mess Hall have sparked my dream? Why would I imagine her drunk?

"Are you having a flashback of the combat after you landed on QM-4811?" The chair righted itself and slid back to the desk. "Care to sit and talk about it?"

Care to sit and talk about it from The Brains was always rhetorical. Getting my heartbeat under control, I sit and recount, again, what I had told them in Big Blue.

Seven

Normally, the worst thing about having Jacobs on point is following in his funk-mouth wake. However, I don't smell anything but the shit-slime on my armor. Stripe and Dixon are jacked in, drawing on my energy reserves but keeping close to the walls as I walk down the center. I can't blame them. The pungent stench is strong and I'm beginning to taste the foul ichor.

I scrape my tongue with my teeth and spit again. My saliva has become white, chunky, and streaked with faint yellow.

"Roach." Stripe points. "That is nasty."

Dixon made a non-committal grunt. "Sort of looks like tapioca."

Though they are causing my reserve to steadily downtick, I can't expect them to stumble through the dark.

Stripe motions forward to get me to look away from it. "Can we not see the next one?"

"I'll try." Their vision is tied to mine, and I give them a view of Jacobs peering around a corner with a *hold* fist in the air.

The longer he stands there, the tighter my grip becomes. He normally pauses for five seconds; anything longer means he's counting enemies. He's been there for ten, which is just about the longest his species can be still.

Chi'Gan have a hard time tracking quick side-to-side movement.

We start advancing.

Halfway to Jacobs, ruddy chitin-covered hands pull him around the corner. His boots scrape the cave floor and accompanies the creature's skittering retreat. How did I not hear it approaching? Flashes of light from our pulse pistols dot the corner, but the scorp has pulled him away.

I run.

Near the corner, Stripe groans and his jack comes loose.

Priorities. I press my back to the wall as I round the corner and draw a bead past two walls closing in a V, dividing the hallway. A scorp's tail disappears from view.

My thumper recoils as I shoot the shrinking triangular opening. Jacobs would rather been engulfed in what Chi'Gan natives call the *Booming-Bright* than eaten.

There's skittering behind me.

Leaving the reloading thumper around the corner for a second shot if the walls open, I spin.

Stripe has been pulled behind another closing wall and Dixon is in a scorp-bastard's grip.

A roaring grenade explosion echoes through the hall and the shock shakes the ground under my boots.

Jolted, the scorp with its stinger in the side of Dixon's neck trips. It utters the high-pitched clicking-squeal when its eyes swivel to see my pulse pistol pointed at it.

I flip from pulse to stream. Pulling the trigger, a line of light shoots from the muzzle and decapitates the creature. Ten percent of the gun's energy reserve drains away, but the squat body with three legs beneath Dixon stops flailing.

My thumper hums and vibrates momentarily, signaling it has reloaded. I take a moment to aim before launching a slap-top through the wall that's closing. Stripe is out of sight.

I lift Dixon and move backward, carrying her to the corner, cradling her so I can view both directions.

A muffled blast shakes the floor and the wall at my back. I set my thumper in her lap and press my trembling fingers on her throat. There is a weak pulse, but I don't know if it's from her or my own blood pumping hard into my fingertips.

Assuring the walls are closed, I dip my finger into her warm mouth and feel under her limp malleable tongue to pull her stim-pill. Not sure if this is a good idea or not, I set the pill between her wisdom teeth, press her lips closed, and use the palm of my gun hand to squeeze her jaw.

Hoping the adrenaline mix will combat the poison and not speed it through her system; I sniff the apple scent coming from her nose. As I wipe white gunk from the corners of her mouth, I promise, "It's not going to end like this."

I lift my thumper and aim it at the walls Jacobs was dragged beyond. I pull Dixon's thumper to train it on the wall Stripe had been carried through.

To conserve power, I lock my joint, halve the flow to my optics feed, and shut off my faulty audio receptors.

I don't know what difference it will make if she becomes mobile, but I wait and wish for it just the same.

Four

Out of the loose cotton iso-orange, I pause outside Mess and straighten my stand-down blue jumpsuit. The rigidly starched sleeves almost make me feel like my old self again. My memory recalls the jean material well, but my fingers register the uniform like it is my first time touching it.

I can hear the buzz of conversations and smell pizza through the small crack in the swinging doors. Scraping my tongue on my teeth, I discreetly spit the remnants of the antiseptic mouthwash bio-iso makes you swirl before being reinstated.

I lean left, then right, to take in the entire hall; it's quite full. The center area is awash with green crew uniforms speckled with yellow facilities and white housekeeping jumpers. The tacticians fill the distant right corner.

I push both doors open and head to the far left corner, where only black and blue sit. They rise and, much to the chagrin of the other diners, chant my handle to welcome me back. "Roach. Roach. Roach."

Green, yellow, white, and gray have no idea what being in iso-orange feels like. They've never been deep in hostile territory, only to return home to face thorough examination at The Brains' perfected passive-aggressive tones.

My squaddies do, and we yell to shake the ship with cheer when one of us returns. When we're lucky, a squad member gets released once a week. When we're not, it means a squad did not return and they wake other contracted explorers from suspend-sleep to suit up in blue.

A bit richer for my find on QM-4811, I raise my arms and cross my wrists above my head.

Another round of cheers. A score means free lunch for your fellow squaddies and keeps the hope of a big find alive. I look to the Pay Warden in green to make sure she sees my *X*.

She nods.

The elation carries me to our corner, where room has been made for me along with a tribute plate with various slices of pizza donated—more than four of me could eat.

As the applause dies, Benson asks what everyone is itching to know: "So, what did you guys score on QM-4818?"

4818? He must be confusing his upcoming planet recon number with the one I just returned from. I lift a slice a pepperoni pizza, take a bite, and savor the dough mashing between my teeth. As is customary, I keep them waiting. After a bit, I let my smile come full force. "Enough 53 and 79 to make the resource meter ping a solid four."

A collective, "Whoa!" ripples through the group. My back receives congratulatory pats as black and blue break away to their respective seats with greedy grins. It was more than an *if it were me* look. It was as though they had scored, too, or knew they were being sent to a resource-heavy planet.

As usual, everyone breaks into smaller groups, murmuring about what they would do with the cash; leaving the recipient time alone with their pile of food.

I always see it as a load of guilt.

The ritual is great, but the relative isolation in the group always makes me wonder who else made it back. I would rather split my fortune four ways than lose a squad member and, unfortunately, I know the rest do not feel the same.

I turn up my audio receptors to listen for those sniggering about hopes of others not making it or The Brains never releasing them. I take notes to make sure not to end up on the same mission, or, at least, not wind up on the same four-man team, as them.

I already know what a four-dot haul means for my parents. Their account would uptick enough to pay secondary school for all of my younger siblings and many cousins. Plus, a decent college for whomever has the best grades. I know who I hope it is, but won't say such in my letter home.

I'm out here working for all of them, and hopefully I'll score better to square them all away. If I hit a six-dot, I'll be able to send my mom a mandate to get dad better legs and there'll be so much money, he won't think to refuse.

+

Besides me, my heaping tray of pizza, and the Pay Warden, the mess is empty. They don't rush you out on your first day back. After being mobbed, it's good to have some real time alone. Though the ship is enormous, it is not so big as not to constantly run into people.

Jacobs enters. He's in iso-orange. Being the only Chi'Gan to join the squad, his jumper is short on his limbs, loose, and has holes cut on the side for his extra set of arms.

He turns to grab a tray and I call, "Jacobs! Plenty over here."

Though we're well beyond formalities, he responds in traditional Chi'Gan fashion. He waves his four arms, showing empty hands, before approaching. No weapons. I return the gesture. I cover my mouth and then motion, open handed, to the table for him to join me.

Dining at a shared table was a tricky matter for the first human settlers on our planet. Food was scarce, and many of my ancestors were injured or killed by natives when invited to eat, as sharing was a bonding experience. An un-bonded person making a move towards a Chi'Gan's plate, even to serve more food, was an act of the highest aggression.

I lift a slice, the last I'll eat, and slide him the rest.

His small eyes round in surprise at how much I am giving him. Unsure, he switches to his native tongue.

"Roach, you are my Alpha. It is I who should be giving you such a hefty tribute."

Though they are grasping some part of our culture, I give him a closed-mouth smile. To show I understand, I respond in Chi'Gan with a stock saying: "The herd was thick and slow."

His arms flash, picking the meat toppings, piling them by order of preference. Still speaking in his tongue, he assures, "My next hunt will be in your honor."

I nod. "And it will be glorious."

He nods with me before leaning close to inhale.

Olfactory is their primary sense, and having him sniff me again, as though it was the first time—after growing up and working together—he was treating me like a complete stranger. I lean away and sneer, "What the Hell?"

"Your scent is weak." Jacobs grabs a fistful of sausage. Moving it toward his maw, he pauses, his eyes lower. "I knew the meat-you well." He then fills his mouth and does his best to chew with his lips sealed to keep his funk in check. It helps, but the musk spreads with each bite.

I drop my slice and check my hands. "The meat-me?"

"The new you isn't bad, but once your scent is gone from your clothes, it is going to become hard to tell you apart from the others." He pulls from a pile of pepperoni. "You know, with you not having any glands or genitals."

"What in the fuck are you talking about?" I turn to force eye contact with him.

Being Chi'Gan, his eyes meet my optics for a moment, but start dipping to show submissiveness.

Faint baby powder is in the air and a click releases an invisible cloud from under the table. The air freshener assaults my nose and I fall away from the table.

A quick scan finds the source.

It's the industrial stuff housekeeping uses to cover any odor. The canister is taped to the bottom of the table. Not a bad trick.

I wonder which of the squaddies had the connections and resources to do this. First, they would have to get a can from White, a timer from Yellow, and then pay off someone in Green to place it here.

I stand and look at the pile of pizza laid on me by the other squaddies. I'm full and, lost in thought, must have been picking the toppings.

Eight

"I know you're confused."

I try to switch on my optics, but they don't respond. I attempt to close my arms around Dixon, but they are not functional. There's light oil in my mouth, and the air is sterile, if not stale. My energy reserve is at one. All non-communication systems are inoperable.

"It's always confusing, at first."

Feeling the stim-pill under my tongue, I bite into it. Instead of cherry pie, my mouth is filled with hot static. My reserves kick up to twenty-one and a BIOS flash resets my controls, and I'm able to move.

I spring from the cold table and, thinking I was still holding guns, point empty hands at the stone pillar with a speaker box on the other side of the table.

"Where is Human : Female : Ring I was guarding?" I try to think of the human's identifier, but only have a vague memory of what apple pie smells like. At a loss for proper words and weapons, I ball my metal fists. "She is my prime root cause. Deliver her or perish."

"I know how you feel." The voice coming from the column rings with a familiar cadence. It is my own, but from outside. "For she is my prime root cause as well."

My sub-routines attempt to cast my optics around the area to take in additional data, but they are locked on the stone column. I run a search query for Human : Female : Ring. My optics respond and scan.

The area is all Unknown : Metal : Alloy. Dimensions are a hundred meters depth, eighty meters width, fifty meters height. There are forty rows of seventy one-meter long, meter wide, tables. A similar stone column stands between every other table on every second row. Each table has identical robots with human anatomy on it in various stages of production.

I archive the remaining details for future classification and use. "Where is she?"

"I know you are having problems with your memory. The Human : Void : Voice has tampered with your hardware and programing."

The stone columns projects a hologram. Each was a Human : Female. All were unique. The only common factor was the Human : Female anatomy. They all raised a hand. All of them have a Ring. Half of them on the left hand, the other half on the right. Some rings were on the same finger as the others, but the majority of them were not copies.

"If you can identify the specific Human : Female : Ring that you are looking for, I will reveal her to you."

A flash of a hand with a finger extended came to mind. "Long finger." The Human : Female : Holograms with rings on the opposable digit disappear. A gesture I had cataloged eighty-three times registers. "Middle finger."

Images with the ring on other fingers vanish, leaving ten to pick from. Human : Female : Ring was on my left when I reminded Human : Male : Waste of his proper classification. She walked me backwards with the ring hand. "Left." Four more holograms disappeared.

"Impressive."

Six left. My fists began to shake. There was no one here I could force to deliver her to me, nor was there anyone to take my frustration out on. "Apple pie."

"Nice try, but that is not a physical description."

"Expletive!" Another memory. Whiskey. I invalidate the word. It, too, did not fit a physical description classification. The Beverage : Alcohol : Robb memory continued. She pressed into me, our arms bracketing each other. Our mouths trying to Venn the distance between us as independent units trying to find and define the center area where our individual states would not matter, as we were one.

Calculating. I leaned back as I had when she pushed into me and then forward as I had when I bracketed her back. Leveling my palm from the ground, I lock my joints and rotate to compare the remaining holograms.

"Her." I point to the only one whose shoulder height matched the Robb Whiskey memory. "She is my root cause."

"Before I take the others away, are you sure?"

"Yes." My facial surface manipulates and moves of its own accords. Classification : Smile. "I am certain. She is Dixon."

In identifying her, I now had the name of the part of the overlapping Venn circles where we were interfaced and are one and the same. The holograms disappear, and a series of clanks sounds behind me.

I turn to see Sarah holding her mouth, tears streaming from her eyes. Excess lubrication forms in my optics. Reclassify : Eyes : Tears. She extends her hands, and I run to her.

Our bodies clang when we bracket, my memory begins to restore, and pure classifications are falling away to true names.

+

They made me and imprinted Todd's memories after he discovered a way to survive and join them. I was supposed to return to deliver a message of peace and commerce. Most of my data The Brains damaged is unrecoverable, but the Singularity agrees my communication of coexistence was rejected. Given the damage done to me, they figured I was a lost cause and had me slated for dismantling. Like the one who I was modeled after; they gave me one chance at survival, and Dixon was the key.

In thinking back on Todd and Sarah's bodies, entwined in suspended animation, I know the missing part of me was not the damage done to my memory banks, but the void left when she joined him. Losing her makes reanimation pointless, and knowing I'm a copy of a flesh being without family doesn't stop the sting of not being able to be with her.

The pain is channeled into a revenge algorithm,

and it takes up most of my processing power when my companion squeezes my robotic hand with hers.

I grip back.

The Singularity says the scorps killed Stripe and their poison did not work completely on Jacobs. With a welcoming mad grin, the Chi'Gan caught the slap-top I shot at him.

She squeezes my hand. The code representing the pain of Jacobs' loss is reprogrammed into vengeance, and I increase acceleration toward the Corp's exploration ship.

The Brains did not want peace and sent all of their squads to try and take the planet by force. Now we are on a crash course with enough explosives to evaporate the entire hull.

It will be centuries before another corporate exploration ship returns, and Todd and Sarah will be long forgotten—yet still entwined.

He has her. I have Death Blossom and a new root cause.

CLEARING CRYSTAL

In a world where magical souls reincarnate, mystics do not fear death. Though infernal forces can consume them, the long wait between incarnations becomes nothing but an inconvenience.

Hunting for him, men killed Vincent's eternal companion. A century later, her soul - about to awaken - lies within a human sacrifice.

Vincent stole the soul's vessel from a demonic cabal, but can he keep her safe?

ONE

HAVING PULLED A HEMATITE TUMBLE STONE, VINCENT Roque rubbed the smooth glass-like surface with his thumb. Vibrations from the jeep shook his body, registering strongest in his ring-clad hand holding the steering wheel. His high beams rocked across the meadow with each dip and bump. A flash of reflectors in the night signaled he was on target for the two-lane blacktop.

Vincent raised the hematite to his fat lip and pressed it against the bloody split at the swelling's center. The cool sensation eased the pain and the stone vibrated, trying to lend its faint healing potential.

"No, my little friend." He spoke to the mineral as he rolled it on his wound to fully wet it with his blood. "I do appreciate the gesture, but I will need you shortly for your full strength."

A pocket of wind pillowed against his face and burst as he drove. He had sunbathed in this meadow centuries ago, when the virgin land was not tainted. Its pure lavender and dandelion-kissed air was now stale with rot and the sting of devilweed.

Then, he had lent himself to the land when the last of the industrial boom was poisoning her. *She* remembered him as clearly as he remembered *Her* and *She* wanted his healing again.

Vincent swallowed hard and pressed the hematite to his breast to battle the pangs; guilt at not being able to lend aid right now and remorse for *She* was clearly dying. Crickets used to sing all night and now, nothing but the demons and their cattle were alive within a half-mile radius. If the hellspawn and their devilweed were not here, he could have the land back to *Her* former glory inside of a decade, but both the unholy community and the infernal vines had roots too deep.

He could feel *Her* form fingers, trying to coax him into helping. The hematite in his hand began to dissolve, allowing his will to remain strong as his eyes watered and heart broke.

Stopped on the blacktop, Vincent was glad to be on something Man-made. He was beyond *Her* sway now and opened his hand to let the fine hematite dust fall from his palm. Tentative, he turned in his seat and set his bare feet on the pitted and cracked pavement. He pressed his tongue in the air and could taste Man's neglect of his creation like long-abandoned webs in a dilapidated house.

Keeping his back to his former friend, he dipped a finger into his spider-silk pouch to pull another hematite tumbler. Having started with twenty, Vincent thought he had pulled too many, but as his finger pressed between the remaining two and a sliver of flint, he knew he had brought too few.

Stone in hand, he pressed it to his split lip like the one before. It also tried to lend him its faint healing potential too. "No, my little friend." He wetted it carefully. "You have a much greater purpose." Vincent set the hematite on a reflector. Rotating all of the rings on his casting hand, he focused on his cavern.

His dwelling was hundreds of miles away in Yellowstone, but as he concentrated, distance became insignificant. He reached through space to pluck a tiny sandalwood–and cinnamon–flecked candle from the nightstand before his knack ended, unwinding his rings. The distance between him and his home was very real again.

Having run the bottom of the candle down the center of his tongue, he began to hum to spread the cinnamon flavor around his mouth while he set the candle on the stone.

Church bells rang.

He looked across the meadow, his diseased friend, to the small infernal village from which he had stolen sacrifice. Though snow was rare in this part of Georgia, the buildings had high pitches and their windows were aglow with infernal light. The intricate webbing of devil-weed closest to the town began to glow the same color before flames rose and licked the air.

Fire roared along the plantlike web to the edge of the road and spread lengthwise across the meadow into a distant forest. The town flicked, flashed, and roared. The high-angled roofs shot gouts of flame, throwing shadows from bodies scurrying through the town, feverously searching for what he had taken.

The fire stopped at the road, but concern speared his heart, snapping his focus and turning his neck.

The mass of braided and curled red hair protruded over the chair, and the sacrifice's pale arm dangled from the passenger seat where he had buckled her in. Her aura took on the red of the hunter's moon.

+

He could hear Carolynn wailing. His lover's cries roused him from his nature bind. Her voice, incoherent through agony, carried her soul-call for him.

The land, which he had committed a year to healing, unearthed him and roots of nearby trees hoisted him to his feet.

He sniffed the rancid air. Flesh and hair were burning. The passage of time had always been tricky, but Vincent stumbled into the clearing on still waking limbs.

The hunter's moon lit her charred skeletal remains. He should have been here for her. Vincent took Carolynn's burnt hand and kissed it.

Her fingers curled around his and she was gone.

+

The sacrifice's fingers twitched. Phantom black-charred skin cracked and fell away into memory.

She was pale again.

He closed his eyes and ran the soft underside of his hand down his face. Vincent gripped his beard and gave it a yank.

The hairs on his knuckles were straight. His rings, brimming with power, thrummed warmth into his being.

Another shake and he was himself again, his magic renewed by the girl who was supposed to be sacrificed.

He dipped a finger into his spider silk and retrieved the small piece of flint. Rubbing the rough sliver, he moved his ringed hand around, drawing arcane symbols lit by the moon–or the sacrifice–in the air. "Fire, favor calls for favor."

The letters became fumes, wavered, lit, and extinguished.

His eyes flicked to the town. The flaming bodies were spreading out, a majority coming his way.

He rubbed the flint again, retraced the symbols, and pulled a piece of dried guano from a domed ring. "Michael," he said and pinched the component, breaking apart the dried sphere, "give me fire!"

The crumbed bat dung became burning coals and Vincent could feel his elemental opposite resist, only letting a slight part of his power loose to fulfill the call, but not enough to help.

The flint blossomed into a gout of flame flowing seven feet into the sky. Vincent released the flint and fell backward.

A shockwave of power rattled his tailbone on impact, echoing up his spine like perpetual force. The blacktop beneath gave, and he found himself in a small crater.

The sliver, which should not have had the ability to produce more than a lamp flame, was an out-of-control conflagration rising higher and higher.

Sliding his palm across the road, Vincent called to the earthen elements being held tightly together–and apart–by the tar. The banality evaporated from the man-made construct, and the earth granted his request, moving the hematite and candle closer.

A spark flew from the bonfire to the wick. It flashed to life. The piece of flint shot away from the town, a trail of red streaking far across the meadow on the opposite side of the two-lane.

Wonder, akin to his first observation of magic, spread through his mind as he stared wide-eyed and open mouthed.

The sacrifice's index twitched again.

He rose. Vincent had hoped she would be his Carolynn, reincarnated, but this girl was so much more.

Two

BEING OF STONE, VINCENT HAD LAIN WITH THE earth for decades at a time. He knew how to be still, but the consistent bouncing would not let him. Always beneath him, the passive resistance of the driver's seat stirred a long forgotten feeling. A feeling he suffered through with his father when he was a boy while they were fishing.

His butt had gone numb. Keeping constant pressure on the pedal had the same effect on his foot.

He ran his hand across his face, grabbing onto an eyebrow and twisting it to welcome the sun peaking over the horizon with a wink. They were safe for the time being.

She stirred. "Where are we?"

"Currently," Vincent glanced to her. The ornate design to her hair, the symbol of her former demon lord's true name, registered again. "Actually, it is best that you do not know."

She shrugged, straightened, and stretched. Her fingertips spread above the Jeep, making visible streams of air as though she was running her fingers through sunrays.

She had Carolynn's touch.

The wheel vibrated in his hands. He returned his eyes to the road. The right side of the car made a humming sound on the thin lines cut into Man's blacktop. Vincent gripped harder, with both hands, and eased back into the center of the lane.

"Who are you?"

"My name is Roque," he answered.

"Rock?"

Carolynn used to call him that. Vincent nodded. "Close enough."

"Well, Rock." She turned in her seat and grinned at the side of his face. He could feel the warmth of her spirit press through his grizzled beard and onto his cheek. "You're not very good at driving."

His mouth took on the same unrestrained smile. There had been so little to smile about in the past century, it hurt–a good pain–his cheeks and corners of his mouth.

"Sorry." She tucked her hands in her lap and cast her eyes at her feet. "I shouldn't have–I mean, I didn't mean to..."

The feeling faded, and Carolynn's grace was gone. A chill beyond the crisp winter morning drove into cheek and soul. "Listen!"

She jumped.

"Never apologize for your gift!" He meant to glance, but her reddish-brown eyes caught and held his gaze. The wheel vibrated in his hands and the tires hummed on the thin-cut lines, but Vincent could not look away. As they stared, the earth faded from her irises, leaving flame.

Was it the fire of her spirit or the investments of the girl's demon overlord?

The Jeep lurched right and dropped. He tried yanking the steering wheel left to right the vehicle, but it made them careen.

Vincent found he was out of the Jeep and soaring through air, an element that–in spite of his sincere efforts and best intentions–never loved him, toward nearby trees.

He crossed his hands, the fingers forming a grid at the first knuckles. Two tall pecan trees leaned, their branches weaving, to slow and catch him. Twigs and bare sprigs cut his skin as he came to a stop in the naked trees.

"Rock!"

Vincent pressed his hands on thick branches and his fingers fell into the crevassed rough bark as he turned to check on Carolynn.

He nodded to the trees, patting a small portion of his power into them in appreciation: a reward for their assistance. They moved him to their lower branches. He raised a hand and beckoned the ground. A small hill rose up to greet him at the trees' lower limits.

"Rock!"

"Hold on, dear." Freshly moved, the dirt was soft and each of his hurried steps sank as he moved. "I am coming."

Vincent rounded the tipped Jeep and gasped at the mass of white bows in complex red braids hanging sideways. A hard slap from his foggy memory. His raven-haired lover was decades lost.

"One moment." The last syllable was pinched in his tightening throat. He cleared the mourning from his throat as he moved ten feet beyond the Jeep's tailgate.

Leaning to the side, he bound the ground under the rollbar and body to his shoulder and then formed another link with earth under the Jeep, connecting it to his right shoulder. He had not tried to move something this heavy before. The closest was moving a stone slab to seal he, Michael, and Carolynn in a cave to be safe–for one night–from the hunts.

Feeling the weight of the Jeep settle squarely on his shoulders, which were melded with the ground beneath, he prepared for the strain.

As he stood and straightened, the earth rolled the Jeep back to its four tires. The girl not only could amplify fire, earth was affected equally.

Righting the Jeep was shamefully easy. Vincent searched for a simpler task to complete, but this was close to the new mark. It was between this and causing cave-ins to crush greedy miners.

He was still comparing when he climbed back into the driver's seat.

She fixed him with her newly red eyes. "Who's your master?"

"Master?" Vincent was going to laugh the question away, but her demand pulled the truth from his mouth before he could hold it back. "I have no master."

"Lies!" One of her freckles faded. "Everyone serves someone." Another blemish disappeared when she jabbed an accusatory finger at him. "Who do you serve?"

I serve Mother Earth is what he wanted to say, but other words spilled. "I am in your service."

She took a breath and the slight ephemeral glow to her eyes died. "Okay."

He felt something in her eyes release him.

Vincent clamped his eyes shut, rubbed his temples, and, remembering he was driving, gripped the steering wheel only to find they were stationary on the side of the road.

Struggling to recall what had just happened and how they got here from the road, he glanced at her. She was looking at the ground outside.

"There's no devilweed here." She looked at him. "What is going to keep us safe from vampires and werewolves?"

"Daylight." Certain time and a similar experience would return the past few minutes to him, Vincent relaxed, "However, know that not every being is supernatural."

"I know that." Her red eyes rolled. "Each preternatural soul has at least four batteries in service."

"The numbers you have been taught are grossly flawed." Realizing his butt and legs were no longer numb, Vincent turned in his chair and leaned an arm on the steering wheel. "For every *preternatural soul*, as you call them, there are at least ten thousand regular humans, *batteries*, walking the planet."

He stroked his beard, recalling the shockwave of dread and fear in his village when the first elemental they had experienced came through. Unlike the other field hands, he had felt awe–then again, he was not a man and never truly had been. "Of which, most have no idea what a preternatural soul is."

"Not knowing does not keep the ignorant from serving."

He gripped his beard and considered her words. "I guess that could be true." He would need time to digest the thought before being able to mount a decent argument. A shrug lifted his shoulders as he stopped fixating on the message behind her words. "Say, what is your name?"

"Crystal."

He had dreamt the name he knew she would have through the reincarnation. "Very pretty." He sat forward and pressed the gas pedal. The Jeep still did not go.

Warmth rose on the side of his face. She must have been smiling again. "You have to turn the key."

"Right." He smiled too and did as suggested. The Jeep clicked but was otherwise dormant. There were fresh cuts on his hand and a few up his arm. How did he get these? "It's been a bit since I drove." Vincent turned his focus on the key, trying to will it to work.

"Rock?"

He let go of the key to face her red-brown eyes; a couple of her freckles were missing. "Yes?"

"Can I drive?" Her laced pale fingers squeezed, reddening with hope. "Please? I have my license."

He tried to ready his mouth, but saying *no* to her was not an option. "Yes, but after lunch."

Her smile and hands dropped.

The warmth on his face faded, leaving an unnatural chill. Carolynn's absence left a hollow part in his heart. This girl, when she smiled, filled the void. When the smile was gone, the absence was raw with fresh vacancy.

Her nose scrunched. "Why after lunch?"

He did not want to mention the ritual he was going to perform on her. He ignored the question and leaned toward the earth. With one hand on the steering wheel, he leveled his other close to the ground.

She touched his shoulder.

Tips of dry grass stretched, deepening to a fresh hue as they grew to meet his hand. Moving his hand sideways, the earth beneath the Jeep shifted the machine up the embankment, leaving lines of freshly turned earth where the tires had been and a streak of spring green beneath his hand.

Crystal's presence had more of an effect on him than Carolynn's ever could. The power from the connection was intoxicating and frightening.

When she removed her hand, the void was as limitless as before, but now took up more space in his soul.

"Okay." Her smile warmed him and eased into the absence.

Vincent smiled with her and turned the key. The Jeep came to life. Checking for other machines on the blacktop, he looked back. Two pecan trees–in full bloom–caught his eye. Was there another earth elementalist nearby?

Searching, he pulled onto the road, into the opposite lane, and was aimed to drive down the embankment on other side.

The wheel twisted in his hands and the brushes of her soft, warm skin over his bloodied knuckles empowered him as he had done to the grass. His wounds closed and he could taste summer in the air.

Crystal's soul was a combination of Carolynn and many others. Vincent had plans to teach her magic, but the arcane mysteries would be beneath this girl.

Steering, she smiled at him briefly before returning her eyes to the road, laughing. "I hope lunch gets here fast, because you're *really* not good at driving."

In the shine of her full smile, Vincent became certain of his guess. She was a Nexus.

THREE

As MUCH AS VINCENT DID NOT CARE FOR FIRE, HE HAD to admit; it did wonders for food. The smell coming from the bread, meat, cheese, and vegetables he held wrapped in white paper with bright colorful print was something well beyond the fish and occasional hare he had eaten in his youth; before realizing the sun provided all the sustenance he needed. The color combination and juices did make it look worthy of consumption.

Crystal wanted a *double cheeseburger,* and his dusty social skills reminded him it was not polite to make someone eat alone. She was most of the way through hers, the crunch of fresh lettuce fading to ravished chomps.

Though she was dressed in a delicate, high-necked white lace gown, worthy of being sacrificed to a demon in, she was still young and was making short work–if not a big mess–of hers.

The heat from the cooked meat had transferred through the bread to his hands and his mouth watered. He opened and bit.

The core elements were familiar, but several unnatural flavors were present. The more he chewed, the more those tastes overrode what he was familiar with. Unable to discern the edible bits with his mouth, Vincent spat the mouthful into his hand and studied the moist mass.

Crystal laughed. "Your face was priceless."

His mouth curved into a smile when he looked upon hers. Vincent extended the burger to her.

"At first you were like, *this is pretty good.*" She took it and set it on the dashboard. "Then you were all, *what is this in my mouth*?" She extended a tiny golden crispy wand to him. "Try this. It's a fry. Uh, a current day potato."

"I do not think modern food will agree with me." Leaving the bag in his seat, Vincent stood on the vacant blacktop lot with its faded yellowed paint. Nature tickled his feet through a neglected crack. The land here was ready to see the sun again, but he had learned pulling away the tar-laden coverings only encouraged Man to lay down a fresh coat and stack *buildings* on top. "Let me know when you are finished."

Chrystal chewed rapidly and swallowed. "Why?" She took another starved bite.

"As long as you go by your current moniker, you will forever be tied to those who named you in service to the one who ordered your sacrifice."

She covered her mouth to speak through food. "What?"

Vincent measured the lot with his eyes and nodded. Between the earth mostly reclaiming what Man had done and the area having a chain-link fence to keep the ritual contained, he had chosen well. He had earth press through the lot where needed in order to get four corners of ground exposed to the noon Dallas sun.

"We have to give you a new name so your past will stop stalking you."

She swallowed. "How can my past stalk me?"

He set the chewed mush in his hand onto the hood. "Think of your name as anchor. You were named by those who bore you." Vincent rubbed his hands dry. "Your name is an anchor to them, the place where you came back into this world, and to those who had dark plans for you."

Crystal crumpled her wrapper into a tight ball and set it on the dashboard next to his burger. "What do you mean *back into this world*?"

She had lit on the part he had hoped to hide between her name and her former master's plans.

Vincent waved off the full explanation. "That will take longer than the rest of the drive to explain, but in short..." He smiled. Explaining this to her, in the same way Carolynn had explained it to him, stirred a faint resonance between them.

Crystal blinked at the feeling and gave a small grin.

"Some souls go through cycles instead of moving on." He motioned to his chest, to her, and then to himself again. "We are such souls."

"How do I leave my name behind?"

He dropped a finger and hooked his last hematite. Empty, the spider-silk pouch compacted upon itself and shrank down to the original web he had used to make the magical container.

Her eyes followed it as it flew away in the wind.

Vincent presented the stone. "We focus your name into this stone. You bury the stone and choose a new name."

"Like?"

He turned away, lifting the stone to the sun as a distraction. "You seek your soul's council in choosing the name."

"Huh?"

Vincent looked back. He wanted to smile, but her confusion weighed upon him and the corners of his mouth. "It is up to you to decide." Raising his hand, he measured the distance from the sun to the horizon. "The name will come to you, but we must get stated shortly."

She had Carolynn's inquisitive expression.

He risked an answer before she could ask. "The sun is nearly at apex."

"*At apex?*" The red lipstick had persevered, outlasting the food and strong wipes with a napkin; it highlighted the questioning twist o her lips. "What time is that?" Her head cocked. "Noon?"

Like things used to be, his mirth affected her. She smiled with him when he answered, "Dear, only mortals worry about time."

+

The lot vibrated under his feet and turned into a hum on his eardrums as he continued walking the shielding square, doing his best to keep the endless power emanating from her bound within the square and into the stone.

Four souls could be transferred in a day, but he had not thought to count of the number of times the sun had come from the east to disappear over the western horizon.

How many souls could one body store?

As usual, in the night, a barely operational streetlight flickered with Man's artificial life. Crystal was still on her back, the hematite on her forehead and her limbs spread to the four corners. He had pinned her ankle-length dress to the ground with stones. There was enough light to see her form and hair.

As it should have, her hair had come loose from the symbol it had been shaped into. The unbraided mass rose higher than he was tall, gracing the air above her.

It was still too early to tell her elements, but something about the way the moon and streetlight played on her red locks as they waved in the air looked like fire. If the girl did not choose air, Carolynn, like other elemental souls inside her, would be held in stasis by the dominate soul to possibly be reborn when–if–Crystal happened to pass.

Vincent had already waited over a century. He did not care to wait longer.

Though it was forbidden–and the most blasphemous thing he could do–Vincent wanted to interfere with the natural course of the process to assure air was the Nexus's predominant force.

Anything to assure Carolynn's company.

However, air would not answer his call to swing the pendulums in the desired direction. Being of stone, he could not fathom what the flighty element could want if *It* did not know what *It* wanted from one moment to the next. Besides his lover's simplest explanations, air was beyond him and he had given up trying to understand.

Aware of weight on the earth, through the blacktop, Vincent could feel a lone set of footsteps closing in. Used to avoidance, he stopped walking, crouched, and–becoming one with his element–sunk into a crack of exposed earth.

Searching for trouble on either end of the street, the packs of humans who wandered these streets never traveled in groups smaller than five and did not consider the lot.

These steps were coming directly towards the lot. They paused outside. Extra force was exerted through them before they left the ground. The weight the feet bore landed lightly on the lot inside the chain-link fence.

"Hello?" A female voice whispered. "With Permission from Roberta Patterson, Mistress of Dallas, I invoke the Rite of Retrieval."

Vincent sneered. *Permissions* and *Rights* were machinations of vampires; a false civility to assure they did not fall prey to one another by respecting territory and rituals.

Had he known he might square off with one, Vincent would have put chunks of tombstones in his pouch as he shared natures' prejudice against the undead.

The voice became stronger. "I am Tsunami from Sweetwater and that vehicle belongs to my Master."

Three sets of feet, which had not been anywhere Vincent could sense, pressed onto the blacktop close to the one who called Rights.

A male voice spoke. "The vehicle and nothing more, or we send your fangs back to whichever Sweetwater you claim to be from."

Uncertain if they were vampires, Vincent wanted to peek to see if they were pale, but it would make him vulnerable. Opting for hope, he stayed hidden. He had learned to affect others' minds and did his best to will them not to see Crystal.

"Easy, Perry." One of the three took a step back. "Can't you feel the demon pact on her?"

"Just making sure she knows where she stands. This is Dallas, puppet." *Perry* was trying to sound sure, but Vincent could feel the man's unease as he rocked in place. "Patterson will bring war to your demon reserve if you try to take anything, and I mean *anything,* but the Jeep."

"I'm only after my Master's belongings and have secured Mistress Patterson's permission."

The three followed Tsunami as she moved to the Jeep. Perry warned, "You have to know, puppet, that demon pact or not, there's three of us. Try to take anything else and we'll explain what you did to Patterson as we hand her your infernal fangs."

His partners fell further back as Tsumani's feet closed on the Jeep. Her weight left the ground on the passenger side. "Oh, that belongs to my Master as well."

"Wrong!" The balls of Perry's feet bore the majority of his weight as he took a step toward the vehicle. "I've been casing her blood for the past week." Perry's weight shift from one foot to the other, and back again. "As soon as the watcher is gone, I'm going to rip into her."

"Watcher?" Tsunami's feet came from the driver's side and pebbles started to sprinkle the lot.

Vampires or not, Vincent went to lift from the earth, but salt pellets–a mix of sea salt and rock salt–landed in the crack where he hid and barred his passage.

Tsunami raced around the area, spreading the tiny nuggets far and wide. She stopped to face the three. "Quick! What was the watcher doing?"

"Uh," Perry shifted again before answering, "Walking a square."

Tsunami's weight left the ground and was distributed through the Jeep's four tires. "Walk it for me."

Perry laughed. "Or what?"

A gunshot.

Vincent had heard something similar in the past, but this was a bit louder than the black power guns he knew, yet quieter than a cannon.

The weight being pressed upon the earth by Perry became lighter and a relatively equal amount of weight was being redistributed, in chunks, around his feet.

Perry's partners' weights disappeared.

More shots.

Bullets chipped away blacktop.

"Slimy rats." Tsunami's feet registered on the driver's side of the Jeep again. They walked to Crystal, lifted her weight from the earth, and carried it back to the Jeep.

Again and again, Vincent threw his body, will, and angst against the pellets.

They remained unmoved.

The Jeep started and rolled from the lot.

Four

Earthworms working through ground containing his spirit always felt like his soul was being tickled. In the past, Vincent would seek out soft soil and meld with the earth to relish in the sensation. The soft, steady grinding of their digestive tracks played on his ears and their constant wiggle worked through him, bringing soil from outside his area. This was his favorite activity as this is truly how time was meant to be passed.

However, being locked in the earth, each worm meant a span of time, turning thrill into torture. At first, to have an idea of how many sunrises he missed, he kept track of worms, but found the span between visits incalculable.

Eventually, rainfall began. Seven light drizzles broke some of the salt down. Not enough to escape, but enough to light his tastes buds–stoking his desire to burst into the lot.

A storm rolled through the area, first pushing a few salt pellets free and then soaking the earth, further diluting the barrier.

Freed into an icy rainstorm, water beat at the dirt on his skin. Aside from the occasional need to clean,

Vincent held no love for water–*It* did everything *It* could to erode his element.

Some of Crystal's presence was still in the lot. Tracking the warmth past a couple of lot rats, he found the hematite near where she had laid for the ritual.

Vincent's fingers brushed against the smoothed mineral and he stumbled away from the power. At risk of being consumed during sacrifice to a demon, nearly every soul encapsulated in her had fled into the hematite.

He focused on the stone resting on the glistening lot.

Though not surprised with the multitude of abilities he did not know the other elements lent to their wizards, Vincent's jaw slackened at the vast array of powers earth Elementalist *could* manifest. Powers he could not see a use for, many beyond his need and understanding; some even called upon other elements to strengthen the caster.

From the brush with the stone, he knew three things: One, Carolynn had not abandoned Crystal–being the protector he knew her to be, Vincent had expected as much. Two, he could devote eternity to understanding the powers locked within and possibly be content. Three, all the earthen abilities in existence were nothing compared to Carolynn's company.

Vincent cast his eyes to the dark storm clouds. Rain still fell, but localized winds were steering the falling water to fall ten feet away from him.

The wind knew what he wanted and, from the rare show of support, must want the same thing.

Her name tumbled from his lips. "Carolynn."

Vincent scooped the stone and squeezed it. Keeping his fist tight, he ran past a couple more lot rats on his way to the other side, where he dove into a large patch of exposed earth and began burrowing back to Sweetwater.

+

Vincent tried to uproot devilweed and failed. He took to surveying the field through the ground. Moving twenty feet under the roots, he could feel their malice and the pain in the land.

The actual vine was only six inches deep, but its essence extended further. With the knowledge acquired from the stone, Vincent estimated the vines took five years to take root, but corrupted the earth upon germination.

As he had guessed prior to stealing Crystal, the devil-weed network extended in all directions from the town.

Forcing his way through the blacktop, Vincent looked across the meadow choked with the coiled yellow vines. He kept from dwelling on memories of sunbathing here over a century ago and focused on how we was going to locate Crystal.

If he was in the lot for two years, she could have reached another sacrificial age, eighteen, and already be dead with their souls absorbed by the demon.

The ritual hematite still grasped tight, he dared to hope and brought his fist to his mouth. "Air, you fill what earth and water cannot." A cold, indifferent wind whooshed past him, whipping his hair away from the town. Tightness, fear of Carolynn being consumed, took root in his stomach, but he continued his request. "If my love, your lover, is in that infernal hole, please guide me to her."

The wind stopped.

Tension in his gut drew into a tight, compressed spiked ball. Trying to make sense of a world without Carolynn, the constriction uncoiled releasing grief, guilt, and blame through his body. The onus of her safety was his and he failed.

The world shifted with his tumult and he leaned like a palm tree to keep his feet in the maelstrom of his soul being played out on the ground beneath his feet. Pebbles were pulled from the tar as the blacktop ungelled like displaced water.

He narrowed his eyes at the town and the earth became still.

Wickedness and a want for revenge filled his being. His healing nature began to fade as sorrow started to blossom into hate. If he could exercise his will upon the universe, he could make his final act on earth be nothing short of a cataclysm for the infernal town.

The *Cosmos* began to spread *Its* freezing fingers through him, willing to grant one retributive strike for all his good work done on earth and accept his soul back into *Its* grace.

Vincent opened his eyes to direct the force and found his beard flowing in the air, pointing to the town. A blast of wind moved him forward and he stumbled into the meadow.

The devilweed writhed and shifted to avoid his footfalls.

Hope, like a sprout of green in concrete, sprung through his hatred. Vincent said to the Universe, "Not yet."

There was reluctance as each finger lifted. The *Cosmos* wanted him back and was willing to accept him in an instant.

This elicited a soft smile. According to the only standard he would try to measure again, he had done well.

The last finger lifted.

Vincent's lips drew tight and he pulled his sleeves back as he started toward the town.

FIVE

VINCENT PRESSED THE SIDE OF HIS FACE AGAINST THE wooden door. Unlike trees, the bolted-together wooden planks did not speak to him. Since they were rooted to the wall by hinges instead of trunks, Vincent was mildly surprised to feel them become an extension of his will.

Even near the heart of the village, where the devilweed did not grow, the reek of its bitter rot permeated the air. Identical two-story stone houses spanned both directions, but the wind directed him here.

He could not remember the name of the type of demon which preferred earthen homes, but was thrilled this town was run by one. The earthen floors and walls were Vincent's best allies. Aside from sound reverberating to him, he could feel when people–or the much heavier demons–were nearby and he melded with the earth as needed to assure he remained undetected.

Beyond the door, like a signature, Tsunami's weight and gait moved; he still did not have tombstone chunks.

He pushed the door open and moved through. It slammed shut behind him. Hundreds, if not thousands, of diaphanous blue and purple pedals showered him. The sudden lively scent suppressed the devilweed and pushed his memory back to a wonderful season spent in Denver, lying with a field thick with wolfsbane in a serene hidden valley.

Vincent closed his eyes and leaned his head back. His mind went to the field, but his head thumped against wooden planks, reminding him where his body was.

A powerful but demure hand gripped his throat, pulled him forward, and slammed him into the door.

His eyes flew open to see Crystal. No, this version did not have freckles–she had dark hair and fully extended vampiric incisors. Moreover, probably due to a gut full of blood, Tsunami weighed heavier on the earth.

"Well, you're not a werewolf." She spoke in quick half-beats. "Let's see what you taste like."

She moved faster than his peaceful mind could think to react driving her teeth into his neck.

The closest he had ever come to being bit was when he thought he was human. He was a boy and discovered a wolf pup in a bear trap. Though he knew its broken leg would make its life hard, he could not stomach its suffering; killing it was not an option.

He spoke to it as he pried the trap open with a stick. The pup's leg came free. The stick broke and the trap closed around his forearm, breaking both bones.

Though not as painful to his flesh and neck muscles, Tsunami's teeth dug at something beyond flesh–his mystic self had been punctured. He felt blood and power seep away with her first draw.

She froze on his neck. Her teeth were in deep. She grabbed at his robes, pulled him tight to her, and released a lust filled ragged moan.

Tsunami's lips moved on his neck, mumbling before she pulled away. The whites of her eyes were blood red and her formerly black, soulless eyes were now alive; the same soil-brown as his. "You're too good to just gulp down," she slurred. "I've got to savor you."

Vincent stamped his foot. The earth beneath her opened and swallowed, pulling her ten feet under the surface. The moment her descent stopped, he could feel her start to dig. He slammed a fist into his thigh. "Why didn't I stop to get tombstones?" It would have held her under like the salt had him.

He had done this to vampires in the past. Depending on the kind of abilities she had, she would, at most, only be under for a minute.

Focusing on driving her deeper, Vincent leapt in place and drove his feet deep into the ground. The stone in his fist flared, amplifying his magic. Tsunami was driven deeper than he thought anyone could be put with one spell.

"Vincent?" Carolynn's Roman accent came from the ceiling. Crystal dangled there by hooks in her Achilles heels, mid-calves, and thighs. The dirty white lace dress still clinging to her frame, but was tattered as though she had been relentlessly whipped before being hung like a chandelier.

He spoke her native tongue. "I'm here, love."

Her eyes opened to the depth of space; her irises were clusters of stars. "I kept her safe and she is coming back, but I wanted to say..." It was Crystal's voice, but Vincent waited with a wanting smile.

A slow stream of white clouds came from her lips, puffing with each breath, and amassing in front of Crystal's face.

Carolynn sounded tired. "This girl is a Nexus, and my time in her, with the others, has alerted me as to how selfish I have been."

"No." Not meaning to, Vincent protested. She always gave more of herself than any elementalist he had come across. He bit his lip. Their last words should not be in anger. "Sorry, Love. Please continue."

The pale vapor became wisps. "I will be near and will wait for you."

With a raise of his hand, the earth beneath him lifted Vincent to the face forming in the cloud. He leaned and kissed the pursed ephemeral lips before the form dissipated.

Crystal blinked at his closeness and gave a weak smile. "Rock?"

Tears stung his eyes as he tried to put Carolynn out of his thoughts so he could focus on the hooks in Crystal. Her heels and calves appeared easy enough to overcome, but the metal through her thighs was a different matter.

He gripped the horseshoe-shaped steel and gave it a shake. "Is this in muscle or bone?"

Crystal grimaced. "Bone." Her eyes shot wide. "Rock, this beautiful woman visited me. You should have seen her."

Still buried, he could feel Tsunami digging. She was fast and now a hundred feet away.

Inspecting the metal, he found the connection joint where the crossbar and hoop had been melted together "Yeah?"

"Yeah!"

Vincent could feel her eyes on him as he pointed to the mound beneath him. It grew, allowing him to inspect where the iron met the ceiling.

The vampire had dug her way to fifty feet shy of the surface.

"She was tall, had long dark hair, and didn't know any English."

"She knows English." Fondness warmed his face as he tried to shake the rod anchoring inquisition-like manacles. It would not budge. "She does not like how her accent sounds."

"You know who I'm talking about?"

His smile had not waned. "Yes."

Tsunami was nearing the surface.

"You have to be the one to ground it." Vincent presented the hematite to her and a lifted column of soft earth. The stone started to heat when she extended her hand and he could feel a score of tiny hands, the souls within, raking against the surface.

The stone sizzled and burned both of them when Crystal took, and dropped, it on the column.

She sucked at her fingers.

"Tamp it down." Vincent ignored his burn and started to turn the rings on his hand, feeling the distance between him and his home draw to near nothing.

Crystal poked the stone and drove it an inch. It sank deeper on the second jab when her fist against the dirt stopped her finger from pushing it further.

Tsunami's hand broke the surface. He could feel air drawn down into the earth. Her chest swell against the dirt as her lungs filled before uttering a muffled, "Intruder!"

The ceiling, walls, and ground erupted; becoming a fire in a solid state. These flames burned hotter than any blaze Vincent had experienced. Not only was his skin roasting, but his bones were like hot irons inside his body. Crystal and the iron contraption she hung from were the only things spared from the inferno.

A scream came from the ground.

Crystal scooped her hair and pointed at Tsunami. "Help my sister!"

The vampire, half unearthed, was on fire and screamed nonsensical jabber as small forms–imps, some with wings–rose from the flaming earth.

Vincent pushed a hand toward the burning vampire and the earth extinguished the undead by sucking the body eight feet under. He turned his final ring and the distance between him and his dwelling became insignificant. "The first word out of your mouth will be your new name." Each breath only served to intensify the heat in his bones and lungs. Gouts of fire pressed through his clenched teeth. "Choose carefully."

His rings unwound. Instead of pulling an item, Vincent hoped, and shoved.

Crystal was sucked through space into his Yosemite cavern and the hundreds of miles between them became real again.

Sets of clawed hands pulled on each ankle and raked at his body. Small pink demons climbed over each other and flapped around him, struggling against their kin to dig at his skin. Larger, deep red, demons materialized beyond them from the flaming floor.

Vincent let them have his shell and relinquished his soul to the *Cosmos*.

All traces of heat and pain vanished. His awareness expanded to encompass the world. He could sense the endless struggles of all beings: the living, the animated dead, and the otherworldly.

He had been one of them, and it was all he had known; so much more now lay open to him. A shade of his former self wanted to see what was happening in a cave in a mountain range, but a force he knew well wanted to explore the universe with him.

The person in the cave had been important to him, but this soul–playful, familiar, inquisitive–was more.

Together, they turned away from Earth and flew.

UNSEEN

In a deadly world of secrets, life in service to a shadow agency means no connections, no ties, and - ultimately - not trustin anyone.

In order to safeguard humanity, one must commit atrocities others cannot fathom. One must sacrifice self, but keep from becoming a complete monster.

In such a world, Kurt Ramsey holds the only job with a life expectancy shorter than an investigative reporter's

???? HRS

I STRUGGLE TO REMAIN STILL AND ASSESS MY surroundings. Though I'm laying, the world ungulates and spins without a discernable pattern. The area smells of barbeque, mustard, and roses. The side of my face is pressed against the moist ground, and the dampness has soaked through my shirt. Something heavy is on my back, and I taste grass. My arms are behind my back; chilly bracelets—handcuffs—hold them there.

The weight on my back, a knee, shifts. It rocks me, but without my equilibrium settled, everything feels like it is being flung from a building. The move awakens a deep throb just above my right temple, sending flashes of light across my closed eyes.

"Easy, buddy."

I must have groaned.

"You've got quite the knot." The voice, female with a Canadian accent, comes from above and behind. "What can you tell me about her?" The weight on my back shifts again.

The world moves more than it should, but less than before. "Please run me." I spit grass, and a bit of dirt on my lip falls between my cheek and gum. I sputter to get it, and a reluctant blade, out of my mouth.

"I would, but you don't have a wallet."

Equilibrium returning, I open my eyes, and pain from my temple makes the right clamp shut. Half of my vision through the left is a horizon of grass. With only one eye, I don't have depth perception, but I see a woman in a yellow sundress laid out like I am. The neckline is bright red with fresh blood. "How about my name and social?"

"Sure. Hold on." The knob of her knee rolls away from my spine, giving some relief but making it a bit harder to breathe. "What's your info?"

"Name's Kurt: Kilo, Uniform, Romeo, Tango. Ramsey: Romeo, Alpha, Mike, Sierra, Echo, Yankee." I try my right eye again, and it protests.

"A military man, huh?"

She's quite chatty. Part of me hates when cops are talkative. It means they know how to casually pry information from the unsuspecting – which I'm not. Overall, it's good. The grind hasn't gotten to her yet or she is still in love with her job and tries, daily, to make a difference. Give me a burnout any day. "Former."

"A Marine, huh?"

She's sharp. I'm concussed; at least that's what I'm going to blame the slip on. Should have said *yup* or *uh-huh*. "Good catch."

"Thanks, and thanks for serving." She shifts her weight again. It's her right knee. She adjusts behind me to keep the advantage but relieve all pressure. "I'm ready for your social."

Making sure not to give her a reason to hop back on me, I scan for the second woman but don't see the jeans or white button-down. She couldn't be the one who knocked me out; I had visual on both of them. "Eight, sixty-seven, eighty-six, forty-seven, seventy-seven."

"Okay." A tenth of her earlier load returns on my lumbar. "How about a real social security number?"

"Pardon?"

"The first three peg where you received your card and there isn't an eight, sixty-seven."

She's the first to pick up on that. "Please, just run it."

While she thinks about it, I try my right eye again. The pain comes back, but it opens. The picnic spread looks untouched.

Her radio chirps. "Dispatch, Unit 5644."

A male voice responds, "Go ahead, 5644."

Beside from typical absorption up the side of the sundress, there's no blood on the back. Whoever got her did it facing her... and yet she still fell forward?

"Please run Kurt Ramsey. Kilo on Kurt, common spelling on Ramsey, and I have a social."

The two chose a good place to meet. Granted, they are a bit deep, but Pogorelich Park is in a business district and very public. However, nowhere is without risk when there are people willing to kill to keep secrets.

The male voice prompts, "Go ahead."

She answers, "Eight, sixty-seven, eight-six, forty-seven, seventy-seven."

"Copy. standby."

I lift my head. The picnic basket is missing.

"Please remain still, Mister Ramsey." She lifts from me. In my right peripheral, I see her slender finger. Clear gloss-trimmed nails point to the body. "While we wait, who was she?"

I have no doubt she is going to eventually find out. If she's diligent enough, which she is, she might discover the nature of the exchange that was to take place. Then I'd be the one asking her questions.

Even if The Power That Be suppresses the story, 5644 will hunt the information down. However, I'm not going to tell her that she has a dead Nobel Prize-winning astrophysicist on her hands. "My code is: Uniform November Sierra Uniform November Golf."

"Wha–"

Dispatch cut across her question. "Unit 5644, uh, the system has come back asking for a code."

Her radio chirps. "Uniform November Sierra Uniform November Golf."

She did not hesitate or ask for me to repeat it. I'll have to remember her because there is no doubt that she is going to remember me.

Two more squad cars pull into the lot closest to us. The first officer heads our way while the other goes to his trunk and retrieves the yellow tape.

"Unit 5644, I now need a pass phrase."

"Well?" She asks.

"I walked the line."

She cues her radio and repeats it.

Dispatch responds, "Whoever you have there has been cleared through the Secret Service."

Her keys jingle and the cuffs press into my wrists. "I'll have these off in a jiffy, Mister Ramsey."

"Thanks." I decide to press the small talk to keep her from doing so. "I thought you had to be an American citizen to be a Police Officer."

"My accent, huh?" She freed one of my hands. "Please place that behind your head."

I do and nod.

"I get that a lot." The other cuff comes off, there's a clack as she puts them together, and a clasp snap when she puts them away. "I'm American, but was raised in Quebec."

Testing my equilibrium, I get to my knees, and my shirt clings to me. The world is steady. I touch my temple. My right eye closes from the sting as I run a finger along the edges to get an idea of my hematoma's size.

Set, I take the next step and get to my feet. The horizon wobbles, but it's manageable.

"Why don't you carry a wallet?"

There's no doubt that she patted me down and did not find my ID. Instead of producing it, I lie. "Left it in the car." No need to give her more to fixate about.

"If I may, Mister Ramsey, one more question."

On my feet, I can see over the doctor's body. Her purse and the attaché case are missing.

This is where I was standing when I was knocked out. Taking in the open grass meadow, I wonder how they knocked me out. There's cover close enough, but I would have heard the shot before whatever hit me put me out. She moves to my left, and I turn.

Officer 5644 is blonde, five-foot-five, and slender, with brown eyes. Given her weight on my back, I was expecting more of a prison matron's build. She points to where my head indentation could still be seen in the grass. A barbeque rib and potato salad sits on the same kind of plate from the picnic. "Why serve yourself a plate?"

1418 HRS

As always, the wood floor in the hallway outside Greenie's apartment shines and smells of orange industrial cleaner. The building is the kind of place I would keep an apartment in if the job didn't have me constantly living out of motels.

Balancing the coffee in the crook of my arm, I make sure not to squeeze too hard as to pop the top. I knock six times. My other hand presses an icepack against my temple and, between the two, keeping ice on my injury takes precedence. I sip the walnut blend before setting the coffee behind me and pulling my set of keys.

Surprise would not come close to describing my reaction if Lori Greene happened to open the door. Like many investigative reporters of her day, she disappeared over a decade ago. Unlike the others, she was a devout conspiracy theorist. In working her disappearance, as a regular Secret Service rookie, I found a treasure trove of information here – so much so that I took over the rent. I knock six times because her co-workers said it was one of Lori's traditions.

Keeping with ceremony, I jingle my keys twice, open the door, and step back. Dust sprinkles from the doorjamb like an evanescent curtain.

Knowing how much of a neat-freak she allegedly was, I avert my eyes and pick up my coffee; there's no cleaning crew I can trust in here, and I never have the time. My gaze falls on my usual footsteps and darts away again.

Eventually, I'll have to make the time.

I step to the threshold, sip my coffee, and perform the last ritual. "You've got a visitor, Greenie."

Respects paid, I enter and get to work.

Dozens of four-drawer filing cabinets, stacked two high, line her walls. They're in alphabetical order by subject from the first on the left of the entry, through the living room, into the second bedroom, and across the den/dining room, where it ends.

Further, there are islands of filing cabinets in the three areas, leaving two-feet wide walkways. Half of the living room's island is also stacked and houses political subjects dating back to the Inquisition. The second bedroom's single level covers any topic related to aliens. The den stores anecdotal information and what she probably considered to be proof.

I close the door behind me, set my coffee where I always do in the kitchen, and head to the master bedroom to take in the massive yarn map. A multitude of colors and pushpins anchor pictures, lists, and scraps of paper to the walls.

Going to the only piece of furniture that I brought in, a swivel chair in the middle of the room, I sit and stare. I have no idea what I'm looking for, but something will jump out at me.

Five hours later, the sun has gone down, the ice pack is water, and my stomach growls. I'm no closer to having an idea of where to start than when I entered. As usual, when I come here looking for hints about stuff I'm clueless about, Greenie's apartment is going to let me down.

Still, reluctant to admit it, I lean back and spin in place, casting my eyes to the ceiling, again, to see if a fresh look will make any of the information up there pop.

Nothing.

I gripe. "Come on, Greenie. Give me something." With equaled disappointment, my stomach grumbles. "Fine," I say to her memory, "I'll come back tomorrow."

I stand, stretch, and sniff like a bloodhound. Somewhere nearby, lasagna bakes. Hungry, I smile at myself in the mirror and straighten my grass-stained shirt. "Wonder if they would mind a visitor."

Making my way out, I backtrack my steps to keep them perfect and wonder if a small part of me likes this place dusty just to play a child's game on the way out – miss a step and you fall into the hot lava. Though I like to think if I miss a step, I cause the collapse of the free world; same game, different stakes.

I open the door, reach for my coffee, and pause. The sip hole on the lid is still lined with the cup, but the hole's edges have been damaged, making it slightly wider than it should be.

My guts tighten as I close and lock the door. The eerie feeling I got the first time I entered Greenie's apartment echoes from the past. However, this time I know I am not alone.

As much as I want to pull my gun, having it out would be a detriment if my hunch proves right.

I opt for my Maglite as I run a finger along a thin, skin-colored waxy line just above my waistband. One of the few pieces of true tech I've earned reacts to my touch and biorhythms. The miniaturizing pocket puckers open. I slip a hand in, grab the rubberized grip, and hope for a gasp from whoever is probably watching as I seemingly pull the long, six-cell flashlight from my flesh.

Nothing.

A muffled click sounds through the guard as the light beam illuminates the footprints in the dust. Aimed a few steps in front of me, the Maglite shines on similar impressions in my usual route. I follow my path.

It's been a couple of months since I've been here, but the set leading to the living room appears to have been freshened.

I didn't go this way today.

Partly attributing it to being what I want to see, I play it off and mentally prepare myself to be wrong when I walk this place, in heightened awareness, only to find my imagination messing with me.

I pause and focus to hear movement or breathing. Jeopardy's Daily Double sounder leaks through the neighbor's wall.

Scanning the footprints into the den, the differences in dust levels are blatant and a faint scent–beef jerky–is noticeable at the entrance to the second bedroom. I slide my index and thumb across my flank like pulling on a zipper; the pocket opens.

Ready to drive my hand in and pull a weapon, I aim the flashlight at the footsteps directly into the room–how I normally exit: dusty.

I check to the right on the inside of the room–the way I would enter: fresh.

Maglite level with my sternum, I step in and scan the tracks. Four clean steps followed by two dusty steps before the corner of the filing cabinet island. The beef jerky smell is clear here, stronger than the lasagna smell, like a bag is open.

The disparity between the recent footprints and the old is night and day, but no one's here.

"How in the hell–" I press my lips together to kill my whisper. There has been a lot of unexplainable tech uncovered as of late, but nothing that would allow teleportation. *What else could it be? Flight?* I light the tracks again. *Then why would they have walked?* I looked to the ceiling to assure myself no one is there, waiting to bop me on the head. Only filing cabinets and a stucco ceiling.

Though I loathed thinking someone climbed without me hearing it, I eyeball the drawer handles to make sure I'm not giving the interloper too much credit. All of them are in good condition, with a thin layer of dust.

My gaze returns to the heel of the last clean footprint heading in. Hoping to initiate, I whisper, "I know you're here."

The area around the ball of the foot widens and there is a slight scrape as though someone pivoted.

I bring my left hand across my chest to block my heart and throat. I turn the Maglite perpendicular to the floor and my wrist gives from extra force as something whiffs over my head.

A shimmering ripples along the thin object deflected by my flashlight. The glittering traces the object–a cane– and then highlights dress shoes, suit, and bowler hat of the five-foot–six-inch person holding it. The slim waist, flat chest, wide-shouldered body turned away from me. Fresh tracks mark his path.

"Hold on!" I hit the corner, but the glimmer is gone. I head back to the door and extend my arms to block the way.

The sound of something sliding past and a streak in the dust alerts me that he slid through my legs and is beyond me.

I turn.

The pitch-black body with sunglasses, wearing a black suit with shiny black dress shoes is rising with his foot planted. The black, silver, and gray-striped walking cane in his hand is extended for balance as the heel of his other shoe drives into my chest.

I stumble back and pull my Stunner from the open pocket.

He's already beat feet, his footsteps pointing into the living room.

I stand in the doorway, weapon aimed chest height at air, leading to the living room. I pull the trigger. Four barbs sing and crackle as they span the distance.

The cane lights with ambient blue energy. The black hand holding it is also aglow for a moment before it releases the item, letting it clack on the wood floor, followed by him crashing into filing cabinets.

He's visible, twitching, and trying to get back to his feet.

I drop the stun gun, fetch another, and aim.

His sunglasses have come off, and there is unequaled darkness, deeper than his skin, where his eyes are supposed to be. He extends a trembling hand toward me.

I pull the trigger.

1939 HRS

I REACH INTO THE BAG, THE SEAL PRESSING AGAINST MY wrist as I riffle through the jerky for a decent-sized piece. The bag crinkles. Propped against the window-sill, I keep my Maglite on my zip-tied-and-handcuffed visitor on the swivel chair and pull a bumpy slice of beef jerky. I give it a sniff, noting the heavy, black-peppered tang, before taking a bite.

Instead of black pepper, something hotter lights the sides and tip of my tongue. I chew and suck at the heat with appreciation as he continues to look away. He's not going to speak first. I compliment, "White and red pepper added to the black." I swallow a bit and cough as it bites back. "A very nice combo."

He glances my direction, at the Maglite, before looking away. "Is this supposed to be a cut-rate third-degree?"

I clear my throat and drop the piece back into the bag. While hungry, I don't want to cough through the interview. "No, this is nothing close to a *third-degree*." I move to the light switch and give it a couple of flicks. "I haven't paid the power in years." On my way back to my perch, I set the bag in his lap. "No, no torture or threats." I smile. "Right now, we're just two guys talking."

"You must know that we are both dead men if you take me in, Agent Ramsey." Aside from his jaw, he's motionless. "They will not attempt to question me. They will kill me and anyone who knows about me."

"Come on." My grin remains as strong as the heat on my tongue and lips. "You know I'm an Agent. I'm one of the guys who knows how to keep government secrets."

"So do they." He shrugs. "Before you do what you feel you must, Agent Ramsey..." His shoulders rise and fall from a deep breath. "Understand this: clearance to know about me, and my kind, is far beyond anything you can attain in the next five to ten years."

Without eyes, it's hard to tell what he's looking at.

"Whatever you believe your worth may be; it is easier and quicker for The Powers That Be to recruit from the FBI or Secret Service than to explain why you, as a *trusted* ENIGMA Agent, know so little."

I try to keep my smile, but the high corners dip upon hearing my faction's acronym.

"Yes, I know." He nods. "I know about slide pockets, swap-spots, and so much more." His contemptuous tone flees as I ball my fists. "Yet you know nothing of the Eclipse."

Though I'm being played, my stomach growls when garlic butter joins the lasagna scent permeating the apartment. They say bread is the only way to extract heat from a searing mouth.

I set my mind against asking about Eclipse. Doing so would only underline how accurate he has been so far. How can I get information from him when I lack leverage? "Well,

Mister Blank, you'll have to give me something or I'm going to see how guaranteed our deaths are."

"Besides our possible forthcoming deaths, we also have hunger in common." He separates his knees to let the bag of jerky fall. "If you order something for yourself and wings for me, I will explain why you need to trust me and how to capture the person who rendered you unconscious at the park today."

My eyebrows rise.

He tilts his head. "Yes, I saw the blow to your temple."

I angle my head to match his and consider what else he may have seen that I didn't. "So, you guys can see each other?"

He nods. "Ask for the wings to be as hot as they can make them."

Normally, I give the detained person a warning about biting me, but something felt off about threatening to knock out teeth I could not see. Close, and with the light directly on him, his skin is a deep ash. His mouth opens to the same pool of darkness as his eye sockets.

Each bite of chicken is ripped away by invisible teeth before disappearing behind the charcoal skin. He devoured the ten wings but thrived on my company.

I've seen the 90s shades before; they surround the body with an energy which foils video-capture devices. A couple of other Agents have them. Setting them aside, I lift the cane. "This is what enables you to become invisible to the naked eye?"

"You have to twist the top." He adds, "However, simply having it in your possession will allow you to see the others."

"Others?"

His lips draw tight and he shakes his head against talking further on the topic.

I set the cane aside, pick up a piece of crust, and motion to his hands before taking a bite. "So, what's with the skin then?"

"Born this way." He motions his chin toward his drink. "If you will..."

I lift his lemonade, extend the straw to his mouth, and watch the beverage draw up to disappear into the small black hole between his pursed lips. Setting the cup down, I stand and lift the sunglasses. "All right. Stay put."

The chair slides on the floor. "Where are you going?" There's a desperation in his voice like a kid about to be abandoned. He's leaned forward.

Before, he was aloof. Now he seems downright clingy. Though I may regret it, I share the truth. "While surveying the park, I tripped over something in the bushes. When I looked to see what it was, nothing was there." I point the cane at our footprints. "There was an indentation in the leaves, and I figured I kicked whatever it was into the brush." I wave the cane. "This'll probably show me what it is."

Brow furrowed, he's gone quiet.

"If you want to say something else, Mister Blank, now would be the time."

Lips pressed together, his shoulders rise and his chest fills with air.

He doesn't want to be left here, but it's going to happen. However, I make a show of turning away.

The chair slides again, and he speaks rapidly through his exhale. "If you think you see one of them, pretend that you don't."

I look back.

Slumped in the chair, he shakes his head slowly, like he just lost his fortune at a poker table.

My guts tighten.

He believes he's given me the world, but all I feel is mounting concern.

I clear my throat again. "See one of who?"

2143 HRS

A SPECIAL ASSIGNMENT AS A GROUNDSKEEPER IN DOUGLAS Park, with its grand gardens, taught me many of the common bushes used for color in parks have had their scent bred out. Aside from the vibrant and potent rose bushes, Pogorelich Park was no different.

Closing on the pink hibiscus and brilliant yellow Forsythia, I rub scratches on my forearm where I rounded too close to rose thorns when I retraced my steps. Beyond them was the clearing where I had been knocked out. A radio chirped. Officer 5644's voice came from ahead. "I don't see him yet." Her blonde hair moved past where I had stepped out earlier this afternoon. "Are you sure it was Agent Ramsey?"

This was about where I tripped. Scanning the underbrush, I see a patch of brush-free grass from where I fell and slid.

"Affirmative," a male's voice transmitted over 5644's radio. I glance to see she where she is and find her looking at me through an opening in the bushes. The man continues, "He showed me his credentials, I phoned them in, and they cleared."

She cued her radio and turned her chin to speak into the microphone on her shoulder. "Copy that, Sanchez."

5644 began to press her way through the bushes, heading to small, thorny plants—and me. "I got him here."

I put my hand up and she freezes. "Mind those small brown ones, they have wicked burrs."

She looks to where I pointed. "What are you doing?"

"Unfortunately, I have to answer with *I am not at liberty to discuss the details of my case.*" I resume my search.

5644 makes a stunted clucking sound, verging on a tsk.

Closer examination of where I thought I fell yields a faint, twinkling box edge under some bushes, like tinsel strewn too deep into Christmas tree branches. I kicked it pretty hard. Hope nothing broke inside. "That said, have you discovered who the woman in the yellow sundress was?"

"Yeah, victim's name was Doctor Claudine Wil-" She cuts her response. "What do you got?"

I lick my lips, drop to my belly, and snake my way under briers to retrieve the shimmering item. Mostly focused on the box, I continue to prompt Officer 5644 into an understanding based upon *her* findings. "Given her profession and notable accolades, why would someone want her dead?"

"That's what I was going to ask you."

My fingers slip from the box's slick, rounded edges, and I am rewarded with scratches across my knuckles. I lick my lips again. My tongue registers the granular texture and benign taste of the dust collected there. I want to spit and sputter but keep the reaction in check since I have to wiggle further.

There is rustling from where she had been. Instead of finding a clear path, she's pressing through bushes and closing on my location. Stifling a couple of yelps, she postulates, "Besides your hastily made serving, there were two well-made plates on the blanket where the doctor was murdered."

Extending both arms, I flatten my hands on the smooth sides and explore the dimensions. The dome shape is similar to the base of a teakettle and has a processed cardboard smoothness. "And?"

"*And* there are two empty purses." Her voice comes from behind me with an edgy tone, almost bad-tempered. She must be getting close to the end of a long shift.

Mindful of the briars, I press my elbows into the ground and begin to slide back. "Two plates. Two purses. One body. Have you discovered the owner of the other purse?"

"No. It's a very common purse, without identification or identifying features."

Clear of the bushes, I pause and close my eyes when a peppermint breeze pushes through the bushes, stirring dust toward my face. I would have noticed if anything planted in Pogorelich Park gives off the scent during my recon.

Without a reply from me, she continues, "Have any clues as to who the second woman may be?"

I pull the shimmering box close and give it a sniff. Just cardboard. Instead of standing, I leave the box before me and get to my knees to peek. A bare black chest, too narrow and with too many ribs to be human, stands outside the bushes. *How am I supposed to pretend I don't see an alien?*

Pivoting on a knee to face 5644, I wave her closer. "I need you to do me a favor."

5644 lowers her voice, too. "Why are you whispering?"

I pull the corners of my mouth back. Does she ever stop asking questions?

She blushes at my incredulous expression. "Sure, Agent Ramsey. What do you need?"

"I need you to dash to your squad car, pretending you are holding an invisible football close to your body." I raise a finger to postpone her question. "It is imperative that you keep your back to me so that I'm unable to see *the ball.*"

Her brown eyes sparkle with questions but she gives a stern nod and asks for clarification. "Where should I take it?"

Good question. She can't drive around forever. "Pretend to stuff it in your locker in the precinct."

She nods. "And?"

I pull my business card and hand it to her. "Call me tomorrow. I will explain why and help you as much as I can with the doctor's murder."

Looking for more than just a phone number, 5644 flips it over to see the back blank. "Alright, Agent Ramsey." She tucks the it away. "Tell me when to start my charade."

I look back. The impossibly thin body has progressed into the bushes. "Now."

5644 takes off like a running back the way I came, an arm tucked across her and the other pumping as she sprints.

An angry sound, like fifteen vowels strung together by hyphens, comes from the alien's location. It changed direction to pursue and stumbled into the burr bushes.

5644 is beyond view.

Another heated string of vowels came from the alien before he kneels to get to his feet. A light *bong* presses through the bushes before there are a lot fewer to look through. It did something to exfoliate a circumference in painful bushes around it.

With a clearer view, the alien stands a little less than six feet tall and has three arms. Its three thin *legs* make up a quarter of its height. Between them, beneath its trunk, are a series of foot-long, fleshy appendages. From the profile, its forehead is elongated, and the face does not have a nose.

It rises into the air on three narrow discs beneath. Peppermint fills the air as it flies the direction 5644 went.

As UNSUNG Agents, we are trained to retrieve alien technology that falls into human hands. A small part of me, subdued into idle open-mouth observation of an actual alien flying away, wonders how many other agents know the *alien tech* is truly extraterrestrial.

The thought frees me from my fascination. I scoop the box at my feet and head to my motorcycle.

Clear of the bushes, I look to where the alien was heading and see a black speck flying over traffic and down a city block.

What have I gotten 5644 into?

2211 HRS

HAVING BEEN TO GREENIE'S APARTMENT EARLIER, THE dust curtain is exhausted. The pepperoni-and-sausage smell greeting me when I cross the threshold is too potent for pizza ordered an hour ago. A hum fills the apartment. Though there hasn't been power here for years, the microwave beeps the end of a cycle.

Cradling the shimmering box with my left arm, I run a finger along the wax just above my waistline. The tech responds to my spiking biorhythms. The miniaturizing pocket opens and I drop a hand in to retrieve a stun gun.

Mister Blank steps from the kitchen with a knife.

I start to draw a breath. My fingers grip at the first stun gun vacancy.

He jabs his arm forward.

My fingers slide past the second empty slot, my mouth dries when I knock the third Stunner from its space.

He points the tip of the knife at the kitchen. "Last two slices. Want one?"

I shake my head. The frantic half-breath I drew comes out in quivering embarrassment. "I almost shot you again."

"From here," he says as he moves back in, "it looks like you almost wet your pants." The microwave clunks open. "What do you have in the gift box?"

I pull my hand out of the pocket, enter, and close the door behind me.

Next to the empty pizza box, Mister Blank points to the reheated slices on a plate. "Are you sure you do not want one?"

Shaking my head again, I extend the still-shimmering box. "What does this look like to you?"

Cutting a pizza slice, he answers without looking. "It *is* a pink-and-white striped gift box." Using the fork, he turns the plate and begins to make angled cuts to turn the strips into small triangles. "Question is, Ramsey, what does it look like to you?"

"It's a sparkling box."

Mister Blank begins cutting the second slice.

I look around the kitchen; he's cleaned. More to the point, I can see that he has wiped. The recessed compact florescent lights shine as though powered. My discarded handcuffs sit on top of the microwave. The floor is still dusty, but the countertops and sink are spotless. I turn and point when the refrigerator compressor kicks on. "How?"

"It is typically referred to as a Solar Twig." Mister Blank lifts a yellow glow stick from the counter on his side of the microwave. "Contrary to the name, it is not powered by the sun."

Pretending the pizza smell proves to be too much for me, I move in to take a couple of the hot finger-food-sized pieces. The triangles popped in my mouth, I chew and examine the small child-sized cylinder. Aside from being a stronger yellow and missing a hole punched at the top to be suspended from a necklace, it is an exact replica of the glow sticks sold around Halloween time. "How long would it be able to power the kitchen?"

Mister Blank looks around, his pitch-black sockets taking all the appliances into consideration. "I would like to say indefinitely, but that would prove impossible to verify." He lifts the solar twig and his plate from the counter. The kitchen goes dark with his exit, and the ceiling light and fan in Greenie's bedroom turn on. He sits in my chair.

I recover my handcuffs, follow him, and set the domed box on the desk. The circulating air quickly begins to wear on my nerves. It disturbs the stillness that has been here for me over the past few years. "That fan was turned off before the power company stopped service."

"It is on now." He nods, agreeing with my statement but missing the point. "The only thing we can control is the speed."

"Does it work on cars?"

"Brother," he says, the corners of his mouth lifting into a mischievous grin, "it works on everything."

My forehead tightens into a frown. There is something lecherous to his normally passive tone. I open my mouth to inquire what he meant. Part of my re-training has me close my mouth. *Never ask a question for which you don't want to know the answer.* "Do you know how to open this?"

He nods. "Turn it over."

I do and stare at the small yellow sticker. As I'm thinking about opening it, the box unfolds with a blinding flash of teal light.

+

I'm attending a private all girls' school.
I'm going to prom.
I'm accepted into MIT.
Government scientists approach me.
I start my first real job.
I graduate.
I solve an equation.
Government scientists approach me again.
I win the Nobel Prize.
I refuse a marriage proposal.
I solve another equation.
Government scientists approach me again.
I solve another equation.
I propose a theory.
I see them.
They chase me.

+

Through closed eyes, my vision is awash with teal, as though I am staring into a blue sun. I clamp my eyelids tight to gain better protection, but the harder I squeeze, the brighter the light becomes. My eyes begin to heat. Something perched on my crown holds a cloth hood around my head.

The familiar cushion of my chair in Greenie's is beneath me. My arms are cranked behind my back, held together by handcuffs on my wrists.

Cuffed twice in one day. Close to a personal record.

Keeping my eyes closed isn't the answer. I open them. The light begins to fade and the growing heat escapes in an instant.

With diminishing hope and mounting dread, I call out, "Mister Blank?"

On silent, my cell vibrates against my leg. I do my best to bend and yell at it, "Answer." It stops vibrating. "Hello?"

"Agent Ramsey." The voice is light and breathy, giving too much air and attention to the vowels. "You have something that belongs to me."

I shake my head, trying to throw whatever is holding the cloth in place to no avail. "And your name would be?"

"No need to drag this out." *His* voice is interrupted by a gust of wind on his end. "Bring it back to Pogorelich Park by midnight or I will skin Officer Davis."

A muffled, defiant, yell sounds in his background.

"You must trust that she will survive the skinning, but not what follows."

"I've already left town." I suck my bottom lip between my teeth and release it. No matter what time it is, I play for more. "I can be there by one."

"Fair enough." He concedes, but his voice lifts at the end and my gut tightens, waiting for the rest. "She will still be alive, but, by that time, her skin and eyes and guts will have been removed."

The line goes dead.

???? HRS

MY FACE IS MOIST FROM MY HOT PIZZA BREATH collecting on the cloth hood. Tinny, canned laughter carries through the wall. I can't place the actor's voice to identify the show and ballpark the time.

As I had secured Mister Blank's ankles together with a zip tie, he has done similar to me with lengths of plastic. Having spent much time here, my mind goes to where extension cords could readily be found.

I try to stand and find my handcuffs have been tied to the chair, keeping me seated. My gut told me to trust Mister Blank at first, and now I'm glad I didn't. I may be bound, but at least I don't feel overly foolish.

Another volley of canned laughter bleeds through and I focus to hear a telltale retort, sounder, or catchphrase.

Nothing.

Pressing down on my wrist, the handcuffs threaten to bite as I lift my butt from the cushion. At least my abdomen is not tied down.

Doing my best to respect her private spaces, I had not touched anything. Readying my plan, I test how much play my bound writs and ankles have from the chair. I roll to the bed and apologize to her memory. "Sorry Greenie."

Violently, I thrust my hips up. My feet are flat on the floor. I curl my abdomen and am up on my tiptoes for a moment before the handcuff strip pulls the chair up behind me. My ankle ties sweep my feet from beneath me and I topple.

There's a poof of air as I land on the comforter, and, aided by the box spring, bounce to lie still on the mattress.

Glad to have the hood for protection, I imagine the wild dust cloud I've created.

I slide my hips to the side, trying to rotate enough to activate my pocket. All would be good if I could retrieve my spare set of keys. The handcuffs bite as I press and twist harder. My fingers slide against the waxy edge, but getting into the pocket is out of the question.

A bit louder than the show next door, a detergent commercial comes on.

I find my head shaking at what I know I have to do. Stuck with no other option, I want to curse but keep my lips tight as my head continues to shake against my last resort.

I press my fingertips into the edge of the pocket and my body reflexively tightens, preparing. As promised, with a touch and a tug, the pocket comes free.

That was supposed to hurt.

"Heh." My lips purse to hold back a sheepish grin. Home Base technicians are notorious jokesters, and I believed them.

A deafening pop stings my ears as a blast of force, from where the techs had mounted the pocket on my waistline, rams into my body, sending me, bound chair against my backside included, high into the wall. I have an instant to consider how much my pelvis hurts and celebrate the hood coming off before I rebound and crash to the hardwood floor, two feet from the soft bed.

At least I didn't smash into a filing cabinet or have one fall on top of me.

Stuff is everywhere.

The contents of my pocket: weapons, tools, and clothing, are strewn across the room. Dust from every corner has been disturbed. Before I close my eyes to recover and let the particles settle, I spy my key ring and, more importantly, my handcuff key.

A pounding comes from the wall. "Hey, turn your TV down!"

+

I haven't had to worry about limited carrying space in over a year. Sliding my first holster, rigid from time, over my shoulder and snapping it in place feels like day one in the academy. A loose button-up masks it and my 9mm well.

Before leaving the bike, I clip my shield on my hip, tuck a one-shot against my lower back, and double check my pockets for keys and wallet. I also press my heel into the ankle holster holding a snub-nosed .38.

A wipe below my right ear and my fingers came away clean. The toilet paper has finally stopped the blood flowing from the perforated eardrum. Not my first time, but this time, the world sounds mushy. Hoping against permanent damage, I grab the striped-domed gift box—it no longer shimmers–and step on the grass at Pogorelich Park with seven minutes to spare.

Near midnight, midweek, the park is empty and the surrounding streets are devoid of traffic. If they–*The Tripods*–wanted to stage an alien invasion, this would be the perfect time and place.

A summer breeze carries a light sent across the park. Pogorelich has the fourth largest rose garden in the United States, right behind Douglas Park; more useless information from my groundskeeper special op.

I'm downwind of the murder scene–at least he won't smell me coming. Though, given the size of his eyes and lack of visible olfactory glands, I'm betting it won't make a lick of difference.

On my ninth step, a breathy voice comes from above and behind. "That is far enough, Ramsey."

Holding the box with one hand, I raise my other to show it as empty and slowly rotate. The alien is up in the air on his tri-disc flying thing with a street light behind him. 5644 is nowhere in sight. "Where is she?"

"Remove, and toss, your guns and phone."

His hands are empty so I mind the discs for any change. They are his transportation and could also be his weapons. "You're only supposed to use one *and* per sentence," I say, correcting him while hating the smallness of it and wondering how to continue without instantly contradicting myself. "And not until I know she's safe."

"Like Unsung Agents." The vowels sounds twist and his shoulders rise. "We do not kill unless necessary." His tri-toed *feet* shift on the discs and the rear two give a glint. "Recovering the contents of the box is necessary."

I crouch slightly, ready to spring. Least to say, I don't think I'm faster than whatever weapon he has, but I'm banking on being able to move before he can activate it.

Removing the one-shot from the small of my back, I toss it aside. "Where is she?"

"In the clearing."

"You want this shiny thing?" I weigh the box, and his eyes follow it.

"Yes, please."

I spin, heave it at an angle further into the park, and break for the bushes; my pelvis pangs with each hurried step. "Fetch!"

He yells a string of vowels.

Pumping hard, I make it to the bushes and continue to sprint down the twisting paths heading toward the murder scene.

"Ramsey!"

Scanning the sky between, I expect him to zoom past at any moment, but he doesn't.

Passing the roses and honeysuckle, I take two more turns and see into the clearing.

He's there, standing behind 5644. Aside from being unconscious, she appears in good health. He has a hand on her shoulder, a hand pulling her blonde hair back to expose her neck where his third hand grips something emitting a blade of light the length of a carving knife under her chin.

Enough diplomacy. I pull my pistol, aim, and leap from the bushes. "Kill her and you die, too."

"Kill him." Airy vowels come from my right. "And then I kill you."

I should have known there was more than one. Instead of cursing, I exhale a condemning puff of air and suck my bottom lip between my teeth to let it slide free. Well, at least he got the hang of only one *and* per sentence.

"And then I kill her."

2357 HRS

I chose the Browning 9mm because it was light. The aftermarket hard rubber grip helped absorb recoil, allowing me a more accurate second shot. Three bright yellow dots, two on the slide and one on barrel, assure my aim at night. It was a five hundred dollar gun that I pumped an additional three into and had put nearly a thousand rounds through. The idea of a *favorite gun* always bothered me, but if I had to choose one of mine, this would be it.

Besides the alien's peppermint exhaust, it is impossible to escape the smell of roses this deep in Pogorelich Park. Taking calm, steady breaths, I could faintly taste both as a constant light breezed rolled through.

Looking down the sights, the three dots lined up guaranteeing me that if I were to pull the trigger, a round would go into the alien's left wide black eye. The left eye is a kill switch for human motor skills; would it be the same for these top-heavy alien tripods?

Given my comfort and certainty of what I could do with my weapon, I thought about what he could do with his. No doubt it is loaded and aimed, but what kind of rounds does he have?

The three discs enabling him to fly are small—it wouldn't be a physical round. Probably lasers similar to the knife his partner holds at 5644's throat.

"We do not want to kill either of you, Ramsey."

His voice is drawing nearer. "Don't make me shoot." I point a good ways right of 5644. "Fly there, where I can see you, or I pull the trigger."

"If that were to happen, I pull mine." His airy voice keeps a distance but does not relocate. "My race would lose an explorer and yours a government agent and a civil servant." He makes a sharp grunting sound. "Useless deaths, all. Just tell me where the box was opened and where you stashed the contents, and we will be on our way."

I didn't mean to laugh.

The absurdity of us resolving this situation peacefully after clearing weapons vied with Mister Blank using me for my most ironic moment of the year. "If you are willing to take a hostage, which you are, I doubt you'll let us walk away that easy."

"Our scientific crew died during landing a decade ago. Your human doctor, the maker of that box you had, figured out a fuel that will allow us to return home."

"Is that so?" Three large dry erase boards appear in my mind's eye..

+

I'm in an office I saw during the teal flash. Scrawled across them, mostly in black, is a formula I have worked

*years on creating. Blue and red markers denote the
endo and ectothermic byproducts. A blink and it's gone,
leaving a vague understanding of the alien's anatomy.*

+

I move my sights to be right under the skull instead
of the center of the eye. "Then why did you kill her?"

"That was not us."

My eyes narrow as I take note of the laser-knife. I
allow my body to turn slightly, taking my sights off the
target, as I look at the three discs beneath the flying alien.
Releasing a hand from my weapon, I run my fingers
across the hematoma on my brow. Nothing about these
guys says blunt attacks.

My thoughts go to Mister Blank and the knob on the
top of his cane. He was free when I returned to Greenie's.
He could have left, but he wasn't done using me. I'm glad
I second-guessed myself. Wanting to nail his guilt coffin
shut, I look to 5644 and then turn to face the flying alien.
"Why is she unconscious, then?"

"That is what my compatriot is trying to find out."

I blink at him. "What?"

"She went limp as I flew to greet you."

A gunshot rings through the park, and my wrist
is alive with pain as the Browning flies from my fist.
Another shot, and one of the alien's discs is blown from
beneath it. He careens out of control, rocketing up and
away in a lopsided spiral.

I look back and 5644 is behind the alien, holding a pistol against the alien's head. The Canadian accent is gone, a strong Boston accent in its place. "Who'd you take the box to, Kurt?" She presses the barrel hard into the alien's temple. "Who opened it?"

The accent triggers another teal memory. She was one of the ones chasing me after I proposed my theory on how we could apply a similar fuel here on Earth. True, sustainable clean energy.

A gunshot blast brings me back.

The alien goes limp in her arms, bright orange fluid pouring from the open side of its cranium. She tosses it aside and begins to advance.

"Was it you, Kurt?" She points the gun at me.

My limbs go cold as fear draws blood into my torso.

"Did you open the box?"

A faint shimmering dot flashes behind her. The alien body disappears and Mister Blank appears.

Reacting to my eyes, she spins and pulls the trigger. Mister Blank is clear of the shot and, using the large metal knob on the top of his cane, knocks the gun from her hand.

She punches him in the solar plexus and sweeps his feet.

Pelvis still blazing with pain, I drop to a knee and pull my pant leg up as she dives for her weapon.

I clear leather and fire.

Her fingers fall limp across the grip and her blonde hair begins to fill with blood.

+

Mister Blank came back with the other alien. He set it on the ground. The three arms and legs lay still. "Ten of them came with tech to trade with Earth." He stood, rubbing his hands and shaking his head. "None of them survived."

By then, I had patted her down. Besides the gun, she carried a straight razor.

Mister Blank takes a knee and pulls a small black objects, which I thought are moles, from behind each ear. 5644's face and body changes into a tall, dark-haired male with enough bulk to make her earlier weight on my back make sense. Within moments, the skin darkens to be the same color as Mister Blank's and the clothing transforms to a suit. He extends the items to me. "Follow these and they'll take you to her."

He drops them on my palm. They are warm, metal, and exude a faint pull to the southeast part of the park. Though it seems like he's on my side, the suit at our feet keeps my weapon in hand. "Why kill one of your own?"

"One of my own?" Mister Blank smiles. "Hardly. He is an Eclipse Agent. They will stop at nothing to keep the world as is, and I am an accident they want to erase."

My gut relaxes. If my instincts were a person, they would be gloating.

He stands. "Can I get one of your business cards?"

"Sure." I holster the weapon and retrieve a card from behind my shield. "Going to call to get the formula?"

"No." He lays a hand on the dead alien. "I figure we could partner up again sometime."

I smile and nod. "Your cane is at Greenie's place."

"Keep it." Mister Blank grabs the Eclipse Agent's body. "I now have his." He disappears with both bodies. A large stone, which is sure to befuddle the groundskeepers, appears where they were.

A formula, involving math well beyond my college algebra knowhow, comes to me and I can see the matter exchange equation behind Mister Blank's *teleportation*. When I try to focus on the calculation, the mathematical equations unravel.

Though I can become invisible and possibly look like anyone on the other end of these magnets, I'm left staring blankly at the stone and wanting that tech.

USED TO BE

Against fan demand, *Lightning* Chuck Wilson abandoned his title as *Ultimate Magus* and went into retirement when his spell-dueling federation collapsed.

Ten years later, Chuck runs a magical pawnshop and lives in seclusion. Still, lucrative offers to pull him out of retirement never stop.

Though the grandeur of the past is behind him, how can Chuck refuse a demon with dominion over his son's soul?

Used To Be

Chuck Wilson set the rubber-banded deck of playing cards on the glass display case full of cheap, low-level one-shot trinkets. He rubbed his steel collar and considered the kid.

Even if the disheveled young man in his green, hooded rain slicker had not reeked of garlic, the golden halos around his irises screamed. Out of sight and downwind, the sad story of addiction could be read in the glowing yellow rings from across the street.

His son would be about this kid's age. Looking at this kid, this young man, Chuck prayed his ex applied part of the hefty child support part of their divorce to educate their son. Marcus never wrote, but Chuck envisioned him in a secluded mountain abbey where he was learning the high crafts. Far away from drugs and boorish magic.

Chuck slid his finger across the glass as if to underline the four items presented. "They're worth fifty pellets."

"Don't bullshit me, man." The kid's breath, a mix of freshly minced garlic and noxious funk, could strip paint. He pushed the deck of cards an inch on the glass. "This is probably worth that alone."

"Probably," Chuck echoed. He pulled a glass bowl of butter mints and two small, pre-counted leather pouches from under his register. Each held twenty-five tiny one-ounce metal eggs and, through the leather, they clattered like dice on the counter. He popped a couple of mints, chewed, and offered them. "Want?"

"You're trying to fuck me."

"You ain't my type." Chuck set the bowl on the counter. If this turned into long-end haggling, he hoped the kid would change his mind. "Fifty's the offer. You want the gold or not?" A small part of him felt guilty for using one of Halo's nicknames to remind the junkie of why he was here, but the rest of him was tired of the smell.

The kid pulled the rim of his hood down, obscuring his face with shadow. "Sure." The golden-ringed irises shifted between the items and the bags. "But I know you're fucking me."

Chuck thumbed the glass-and-ruby ring on his forefinger, waking the magic in case the kid got squirrelly and decided to sweep everything on the counter. "They say knowing is half the battle."

The kid snatched the pouches and stomped to the door.

Trying to keep from tipping his hand, Chuck pulled out a fistful of mints and popped a couple more. "Have a nice day."

"Fuck you very much." The doorbell went nuts when the junkie slammed the door open and stalked into the streets of Las Vegas.

The young man was gone, doubtlessly hunting for a dealer. No need for further pretense. Chuck dropped the mints in the bowl to scoop the deck from the glass.

He discarded the rubber band. The cards were the old jobs. Big faces, no numbers, and full of energy. He hungrily thumbed the worn cardstock.

They vibrated.

He turned and spread the cards on air. They lay flat as though spread across felt. He scratched his salt-and-pepper muttonchops with both hands, then held his face. "Victor Mauger's."

The door swung closed, making the bell ring again.

Chuck estimated the mundane deck was made in the 1870s. He plucked the ace of spades and scanned it. He wanted to know when the deck was re-made with magic.

"Uh."

Chuck jumped out of his seat. The ring flared a quick stroke, bathing his pawnshop in red. He aimed his fist at the body inside the doorway. "Fuck off, goldie."

There was a kid there, but this one was clean-cut, in an orange suit with a white shirt. Besides the color, the blazer had a school uniform cut to it. About to unleash, Chuck grabbed his wrist and willed the ring to hold the spell.

It glowered red with Argosian energy.

"Whoa." The kid pointed an orange-gloved finger. Fearless. Clueless. The kid strode to the counter to get a closer look at the ring. "Cool trick. How does it light?"

Chuck blinked at his exuberance.

Hands on the counter, the kid leaned side to side, trying to get another angle besides the business end.

Confused, habit directed his fist. Chuck kept the raised ruby skull aimed.

Hidden by illusion and protected by compulsion, no one walked into The Kitchen Sink unless they meant to and had business. This kid was here for a purpose. "What do you want?"

The kid continued as though Chuck hadn't said anything. "I'm just learning about the different energies. I can't discern hues yet, but that feels like Argos." He extended his gloved hand to touch it. "Is that Argos?"

Chuck sprang from his stool and slid away from the kid's reach. "How about you stop stroking me and tell me what you want?" He bumped through the floating cards, which fell to the floor. Under the noise of the chair falling, he stepped on a switch to signal his guards.

The kid loaded a handful of mints and began to chew.

His guards should have teleported in by now. Chuck leaned his head to the side to crack his neck. The pops did not ease his growing tension. He stepped on the switch again.

Though physically a teen, Chuck began to suspect he was dealing with a much-older soul. Kids don't have this kind of moxie. "You didn't come in with anything in your hands, so you ain't selling. And you're not looking around, so you ain't buying." He motioned his head to the door. "It's talk or walk."

The kid's playful tone fled. "You're a Used-to-be, right?"

Used-to-be. Chuck hadn't heard the term since the World Dueling Federation collapsed. Too much corruption for the duelists. Too many deaths for the viewers. Instead of joining the still-active Sport Dueling League, the hardcore WDFers refused to play by their pussy rules and called themselves Used-to-be'ers for when the sport used to be dangerous.

Chuck had thought about transitioning to the SDL, but there was no way in Hell he was going to dress in one of those God-awful costumes. What little reason he had left was swept away by his wife, along with their savings… and the bitch had the audacity to sue for support.

"I happen to be in need of a Used-to-be." The kid grabbed another handful, leaving a few strays tinkling in the bowl.

The term used to stand for integrity and will. Ten years removed, and coming from this kid's mouth, it sounded pitiful. His minty breath wafted across the counter. A magic was hidden on the current, and Chuck wondered if he would still rage like he did in the old days.

He shook his head and repelled the enchantment. "Not interested, but I can give you the names of eight guys who'd jump—"

"I do not want them." The kid retrieved a large black pearl from his pocket. "I cannot use them." He set the pearl on the counter and rolled it down the glass to Chuck. "Also, I do not have leverage on them."

Though he wanted to let it roll off the counter, onto the floor, to gather dust wherever it came to rest, the pearl emanated a familiar feeling as it rolled closer.

Chuck stopped it.

The pearl rebounded to the kid's hand.

Chuck's palm went numb. Though the chill went through to his soul, he tried to rub it warm.

"Good," The kid said. His grin widened as he considered the pearl. "You are interested."

+

Though he thought he had no love for Amanda, Chuck had been in love with her. They had met shortly after he set record time and accuracy on the Juniors' course at the World Dueling Federation's expo. They shared good and bad times. Their love made Marcus– the only person he would do anything for. She may have effectively robbed him, but she deserved better than that.

Her recipe for lasagna with sliced Italian sausage came to mind. Chuck licked his lips.

Feeling her trapped within the small prison stoked his will in ways forgotten. Sensitivity returned to his hand as his full power came to his fingertips before the collar around his neck warmed – reminding him of its throttling effect.

The limiter helped Chuck focus on the kid. "You're sadly mistaken if you think I give a shit about her." He hoped his bluff worked.

With a shrug, the kid dropped the pearl in the mint bowl. It gave a tinkle as it landed and knocked into the reaming mints. "Flush her. I don't care. She's a gift." He smiled. "A down payment, if you will."

Chuck's stomach sank and went cold. There were few creatures that considered souls currency, and none of them were good news. If Amanda was a down payment, what would be the payoff?

Thinking about avenging Amanda shifted his intentions from defense. The ring–the collar's override–dimmed accordingly.

Chuck smirked at the irony. When the end of the WDF became apparent, Amanda had insisted he take advantage of the dissolving league-sponsored retirement plan before the organization disintegrated. It paid out a hundred thousand gold per rank to retirees in exchange for accepting an enchantment that neutered their offensive capabilities. Nearly two million richer; Chuck's old match-collar now kept power output just below league standards.

She talked him into it. She took the coin and left. And now, he could have used his former power to banish – if not destroy – this extraplanar creature.

"So." Chuck returned to the stool, stood it up, and plopped on it. "What?"

He purposefully looked into the kid's eyes. He thought he had before, but could not remember. Focusing on where the eyes should have been, Chuck pierced the illusion and stared into empty sockets.

The true visage uncovered, Chuck wished the kid's face would return.

"After being dealt a grievous blow, one that would find me the victor of our millennia-old conflict, she ran to the material plane." Its clothing had not changed, but a skull wreathed in black flame floated above the orange suit's neckline. Its teeth remained closed. When it spoke, its words echoed in Chuck's brain. "I have tracked her to Pepperjacks. She must have asked for sanctuary because I cannot enter the building."

The battles of Heaven and Hell were said to always be raging beyond the mortal realm. Chuck wondered if the loss of one Archon would register.

Careful not to touch the pearl, Chuck ate the remaining three mints and put the bowl away. "What's my back-end payment?"

"Your son's soul."

Chuck snaked his arms out and seized the creature's lapels and pulled it in. "Outsider, if you—"

The jacket went limp in his hand.

Missing a coat, the rest of the clothes appeared ten feet back from the counter. The smoldering skull floated above the shirt. "He came to a compatriot of mine." It hooked its orange-gloved thumbs under its orange suspenders. "He's clever, but foolish enough to think he can outsmart a devil."

Chuck began to wind the coat into a tight ball. While not a vulgar display of power, the instant dimensional spell signaled to Chuck that the skull was out of his league.

To scratch an itch, Chuck imagined the quick, one-sided battle between him and it–if he were not under a limiters.

Picturing Marcus safe—and the skull extinguished and shattered—Chuck dropped the coat. He pulled a small leather pouch normally reserved for one to five gold pellet deals and retrieved the pearl with the bag. He pulled the drawstrings. "How do I know you won't just go after my son again?"

"We cannot initiate." The skull strutted over and scooped up his coat. "However, we cannot help it if he comes back to us."

Chuck gave it some thought. He stroked his bald chin. For the first time in a decade, he began to miss his full beard all over again.

"Pepperjacks," Chuck sighed. It was Amanda's favorite supper club. "What's my part?"

Chuck imagined the boy giving a wicked grin as the devil closed in. "It all starts at the front door..."

+

Pepperjacks had been a nice, secluded two-story speakeasy-themed restaurant on a large plot of land. Now a wide, forty-story hotel with searchlights combing the sky, it was a bona fide Las Vegas landmark. The marquee claimed it was a sheikh all-suite hotel and dance club.

Much of Las Vegas had changed in the last ten years.

As Chuck's fame quickly slipped, so had his social interactions. If it wasn't for weekly trips to the grocery store, he would have completely gone from curmudgeon to hermit. Given the number of bodies celebrating life, Pepperjacks was on the long list of places he'd be avoiding on a hot summer night.

The valet, in his Pepperjacks t-shirt and shorts, waited until Chuck walked away to park his car.

Where one entrance had been were three sets of wooden double doors with oval stained glass in the center. Walking to them, you used to be able to smell steak; now perfumes and colognes dominated the air. Most strong enough to taste.

One of the five black suits motioned Chuck to get in line.

Chuck looked at the line of scantily clad women and men extending to wrap around the corner of the building.

He continued forward.

The motioner extended his palm toward Chuck and spoke loudly. "If you aren't on the list, you have to get in line."

Chuck checked behind him.

He was the only one who had moved to enter. Prior to being told, everyone else peeled away to get in line. Chuck set his mind to fight his way through if the skull's claim to know the highest guy on graveyard were false. "Artimus is expecting me."

"Your name?"

"Charlie Wilson."

The doorman looked Chuck from head to toe as he called Artimus over his radio. "He'll be on his way out."

Chuck nodded his appreciation.

The doorman narrowed his eyes at Chuck's neckline.

Chuck did his top button to cover the collar.

Too late. "Would you happen to be Lightning Chuck, the duelist?"

A couple of the other nearby doormen turned to look. "Yeah."

The doorman snapped his fingers then extended his hand. "Loved all your matches, sir. Didn't miss one of them."

Chuck hesitated. He might have to face this guy and his coworkers later. It would be good if they were reluctant to engage him.

The World Dueling Federation had put its duelists through several public relations curriculums over the years. He called upon the training. Instead of just shaking the former fan's hand, Chuck clasped forearms in the old WDF way. "What was your favorite format and match?"

The center set of doors opened. "Artimus is waiting for you inside L.C."

Chuck figured he would be frisked and left his spells at home. They were going to let him in without a pat down; he had disarmed for no reason.

"I'll have an answer for you when you come out."

Behind him, Chuck could hear the doorman asking the others for their opinions. He nodded to the group and moved through. His ears were assaulted by bass thumping on his eardrums and treble trying to drive through his skull.

Chuck covered his ears. The volume dropped, and his eyes began to adjust to the club's darkness.

Something big moved at the far end.

If he had not been told Artimus was an eight-foot tall, black-coated minotaur, Chuck would have moved back into valet. As it was, Chuck had been prepared.

Coming toward him, Artimus flashed a caster's bag, small in the minotaur's massive hands, and then tucked it in his armpit. Artimus was ready for him, too.

Artimus escorted Chuck between the plush booths–the only detail Pepperjacks management had maintained through the remodel–lining the large dance floor.

Walking right behind the minotaur, Chuck made sure not to run into him, but also took in the spectacle. Outside, it appeared to be a human-only venue. Inside, all races were speckled throughout the club. Both half sizes and half-breeds were present, too. The only singular creature was a Piute catfolk, who normally don't come to town.

Moving quickly, Artimus shuffled to the side.

Chuck followed suit, barely avoiding a dwarf rushing through with six mugs. "Excuse me, Miss."

A few steps later, Artimus asked, "How did you know that was a girl?"

"The men have thicker beards."

+

Artimus had stashed Chuck away in a ten-by-ten soundproof private booth overlooking the dance floor. The seats here were as comfortable as his memory recalled the lower booths being. There was a cheese and cracker plate laid out.

Chuck partook as he started to work. Bag on the table, he turned his back to the glass and started going through the wands, trinkets, and totems.

As though it was hastily made of several stolen smaller bags, this was a true grab bag of spells. After the fifth duplicate, he became less disappointed with matching spells as he was with the lack of good three or four-stone spells.

But he could make it work.

Having removed his dress shirt, Chuck spoke his mantra while loading the better stuff into the various pockets and tie-downs on his World Dueling Federation harnesses. "I am the magic. These are the spells."

As long as the foci were touching his skin, he could channel magic through them and cast the desired spell.

He left most of the crap in the bag and waited for Artimus to return.

Before, his mind would be full of arcane symbols and words. Now the only spells he bothered to memorize daily were the ones he could not cast; like picking at a scab to salt the wound.

If the limiter wasn't around his neck, this would be a walk in the park.

Chuck began to wake his chakras. "I am the magic. These are the spells."

+

Chuck put his last small stack of cheese and crackers in his mouth and followed Artimus. There was just something about jogging behind a large clopping minotaur that instilled Chuck with a sense of security.

The dueling format he liked the most growing up, Meat Shield, was no longer sanctioned by the time he rose to prominence in the WDF. They had a similar format with conjured creatures, but they weren't the same as fully thinking/reacting allies capable of offering tactics on the fly.

"I am the magic. These are the spells."

Music, heavy on bass, followed them from the private booth into the elevator, where they encountered a noxious pile of puke. It made Chuck's stomach rumble, and he turned to face the wall furthest from it.

He decided. Despite its minor plus of bringing races together, nightclubs were nasty things.

Chuck blocked it out. He blocked it all out.

He focused squarely on Artimus's back as though it were the stadium wall about to give way to combat.

Hallway after hallway.

Turn by turn.

Chuck kept his focus until they entered a room and Artimus sidestepped.

Mind back in the day. Chuck was ready for anything. Anything but this.

Chuck was expecting a *holier-than-thou, feel my wrath kind of presence.* Or perhaps a *how dare you mortal* or *nothing limits me but the grace of God.*

He didn't get anything close to it. What lay before him in a plain hotel room was a horribly beaten opponent.

She lay on her good side. The worst of her bruises were exposed to anyone entering the room and to allow for quicker natural healing. The room smelled of fresh rain.

The side of her light blue face was swollen from two separate blows. Her silver breastplate had been eaten through in multiple parts by acid. She was missing a leg, and a wing had been cut down to a stub. Her eyes were open, fluttering back toward her brain. The only magnificence untouched was her white hair, which draped over the side of the bed like white linen or spider silk.

Artimus shot Chuck an expectant look.

Chuck could see, in the bovine eyes, that Artimus was willing to defend Chuck from whatever may try to keep him from murdering this still majestic creature, but the minotaur was no more capable of killing her than Chuck.

Being manipulated by the same extraplanar creature kindled a kinship. Chuck asked, "What is her adversary holding over your head?"

"My life," Artimus admitted, dropping his gaze.

Silent, Chuck waited.

Artimus continued, "My long natural life would have been cut short. I was trapped in the building when the steakhouse burned down." He then asked, "What does it lord over you?"

"My boy's soul." Knowing that he was going to fail his son, Chuck tried to swallow a lump. He did not dare to let the swell rise because of the hundreds of broken promises it kept suppressed. *I will always keep you safe*, he had promised Marcus as a toddler. *Daddy will go to Hell and back.*

Like everything else that did not go as planned, Chuck tried to shift the responsibility from himself. Marcus was foolish enough to dance with a devil. Why should a divine being pay the price for his arrogance?

To Hell and back.

Chuck gathered his wits and stood tall. "Pick her up."

Artimus shook his head. "I can't kill her."

Chucks mouth became a grim line, parting just far enough to let the words slide through. "Go lift her."

The minotaur did as commanded. "Now, lead me back to valet."

Those celebrating Saturday night at Pepperjacks stopped dancing and laughing as Artimus carried the archon through the dining booths.

Chuck followed.

The music stopped.

A small voice came from the dance floor. "What are they doing?" Chuck looked there to see an elf shush the catfolk. "We can't let them do that."

The elf leaned down and lifted the catfolk from the dance floor. She struggled to cover the muzzle. "That's Lightning Chuck."

The catfolk stopped fighting.

They got to the door. Chuck patted Artimus's shoulder. "She needs to be visible, but keep her inside."

The minotaur nodded.

Chuck stroked his ring and stepped into valet.

The devil in the orange suit stepped from behind a car. He had his kid -ace back on. "Give me her body."

"Marcus's and Artimus's soul-pearls first."

"You are in no position to bargain, Chuck."

"You've got it backward." Chuck jabbed a thumb over his shoulder. "I have the body and you have two pearls. So, long as the souls are in the pearls, they aren't going to Heaven or Hell."

"Very shrewd." The boy's brow drew into a knot. "I give you one pearl. You give me the body. I give you the other pearl."

"No deal."

"I cannot trust you with both pearls and the body."

"You'll have to. Because, until you do, her body is under my protection."

The boy laughed and laughed, rising to a hearty guffaw. As he did, his voice took on an otherworldly echo. He started to grow. The skeleton wreathed in black flame grew ten feet taller. It ripped the clothing away, and the boy's face faded.

To Hell and back.

Chuck leaned his neck to the side, eliciting several pops. "Come at me."

Five laughing skulls appeared from the skeleton's abdomen.

Though an advanced evocation, Chuck recognized the base spell. He touched one of the low-level trinkets and channeled power into it. The spell activated.

The five laughing skulls shattered and turned to smoke before hitting him.

Chuck aimed his ring and shot.

The skeleton swung its hand to reflect the spell at Chuck.

They both became bathed in red light. Chuck had not attacked but had shot a tether to initiate a battle of wills.

Laughter erupted from the skeleton.

Weight pulled at Chuck's knees, hips, and shoulders, commanding him to break.

The mirth rose into a ruckus. "And this is how you will be remembered. The fool who challenged a devil."

Chuck dropped to a knee.

"Even the greatest mortal wizard is nothing compared to the power of the beyond!"

Chuck's other knee gave.

The fiery skeleton continued to laugh.

Chuck dug in his pocket. His hips moved back, planting his butt on the ground. Chuck retrieved his wife's pearl and could feel her struggling to help him. More importantly, his insides went numb and he became oblivious to the weight pressing on him.

The skeleton stopped laughing as Chuck started getting back to his feet.

It ran the line of energy, raising its claws. "Die!"

His ring seared his flesh as it recoiled slightly before launching Chuck forward in the blink of an eye.

He broke through the skeleton, sending fragments of bone every which way.

Chuck rolled and spun on his knee.

Where the skeleton had been, a fiery teal form hung in the air where the bones were. The flames turned teal, billowed blue smoke, and vanished.

+

Chuck popped a mint into his mouth and hung up the phone. He had been speaking to his ex-wife about the feverish coma she had been in while Marcus was away at a Sport Dueling League expo.

Amanda recalled everything as it happened, but for her, it felt like only a dream that started with her giving up her soul for Marcus to be a bigger star than his father.

Chuck sat in his wicker stool and happily drummed on the glass while looking over his newly acquired, yet incomplete, chessboard. Each piece held enough energy for a low-level spell. According to his research, if all the pieces were placed on the board, the owner would be granted a wish.

He had no plans on completing the set.

If Marcus advanced at the expo, he would go watch his son. And, if asked, be his coach... even if it meant wearing one of those God-awful costumes.

TOMORROW: HUMANITY

Extra

TOMORROW: HUMANITY

JOHN PADRE'S STOMACH GURGLED, FLIPPED, AND FLOPPED. Intense cramps dropped him to his knees and he gripped his abdomen. "How could I have cheated on you, Missy? We aren't even dating."

"Who took your many pieces and stitched you back together?" Missy dropped the needle gun, a weapon she often used to issue vaccinations to the local strays. It clattered.

John's nose filled with the scent of fresh fish from the Keys Fisheries Market and he craved a fillet. "Want to talk this out over sushi?"

"Huh?" Missy shook her head and pulled a bright orange tri-barreled shotgun from the table in response. The weapon was longer than she was tall. By all rights, it should have made her fall over. She leveled it at him. It whirled to life in her hands. Each barrel broke apart and expanded to form off-yellow balls of light in the center. "Who then, instead of letting you die, took those sewn parts, put them in a regenerative vat-bath, and saved your ungrateful, unworthy life?"

John typically gauged how pissed he made her by how high her voice went. Her pitch neared a record.

His concern should've been equally heightened, but just thinking about sushi eased the cramps. A bird landed on the high skylights and stole his attention.

Nearing the height of her range and rant, she posed a question to him.

Normally, John would have been paying full attention and trying to calm her before her rage built, but he was unable to focus. He missed the transition, but Missy's very lucid anger at him had changed course somewhere and turned into a rant about the *insignificance and indifference of humanity and the human race* and how he—and them—only needed *a swift lesson to quickly straighten out.*

He didn't quite understand her question. Not that it mattered; his answer would probably be wrong anyways. Instead, he posed a question of his own. "Are you turning me into a cat?"

It stopped her cold. Her pitch dropped. "What?"

"I can't focus. I want fish. The bird. The—" His eyes went to the tip of her braid as it swished by her hip.

She grabbed her hair.

He forgot what he was saying.

"No, that was supposed to inoculate before I slingshot you into the future."

He remembered his question. "Are you turning me into a cat?"

Missy scooped the needle gun from the floor. She looked across her table of specific-purpose guns to an identical weapon with *4JP* on the handle. She sighed, "Yes."

"Oh, good." John licked his lips. The area of Missy's secret laboratory began to grow in perspective as he shrank. It was better than being sent into the future again.

"You're not getting off so easy, John." Missy pointed at her morphed ex-boyfriend. "I'm going to reverse the metamorphosis and send your cheating ass into the future without a tether!"

John meowed at her.

Frustration forgotten, she pursed her lips. Then she opened a can of tuna.

MORNING GLORY

Extra

.

Morning Glory

"Brother, how could you?" Pain lanced through his right side. Alarick Brightblade cradled his numb left arm to his chest, winced, and cried out.

In honor of his sixtieth name day, the aristocracy of his kingdom had regaled all night in the high spires. The rising sun threw their shadows on the glass-enclosed ballrooms like ants trapped in amber. His voice drowned the revelry coming from the streets. Had there been anyone still alive in his court, they surely would have thought him pathetic for such a cry.

As it was, the only ears to bear witness to his moment of weakness were his own.

The bladders and bowels of the dead had emptied to fill the room with the stench of fresh bodies and filth.

Against his will, blood ran from his nose.

Childhood memories played behind his dull grey eyes as he sniffed to draw the fluid back like snot and mewed in agony.

Weary, he could not pull his slack jaw shut and resigned to letting the salty crimson run down the curve of his lip and creep into his mouth.

Tucking the thumb of his useless arm into one of the gashes in his blood-slicked leather armor, Alarick slowed the flow of fresh crimson from where Clark, his twin brother, had gifted him with rapid knife wounds to the gut and chest in closed court. The *blade* used was crafted from foreign wood and magic; the lumber made the wound, the magic slowed his joints.

Unlike Alarick's, age showed around his younger brother's hard eyes. *Long live the King*, Clark said, drawing close. *Long be His reign.*

What remained of the length of leather to assure the King's blade did not stray too far from his wrist broke. The ringing clatter of Alarick's longsword, his birthright, died on the stone dais across his parrying dagger.

Like on the night he usurped them from his father, both blades shone with blood. The once-brown leather grips were now reddened with the life of duplicitous family, untrue friends, and vile traitors.

The tight-winged bat pommels were the only part of the weapons to show the genuine, bright moon-metal gifted centuries before from the last of the Elven smiths. Alarick wondered if they would forever be bats or reshape to show the house animal of the next person to wield the blades.

"*Long be His reign.*" Alarick looked at his grey-haired brother's body at his feet. He wanted to stomp the skull in, but conserving blood was vital. "There are no more Brightblades," he whispered to the corpse. "You've doomed our name."

The distant music died as the sun crawled higher over First Light's Peak. The ballrooms became still gossamer glass boxes.

Kissed by the sun, the intricate metalwork of the gilded fairy flower-lamps on the far side of the room began to glow. No longer dormant, the pale ghostly lights within began to turn amber.

Enchanted to anchor non-fey *in bloom*, they leaked pollen and the nearly forgotten scent of honeysuckle when touched by the rising sun.

Clark must have activated them.

It was supposed to be a royal secret. A secret passed from father to first-born son. Alarick had been betrayed by blood from both sides of the grave.

"It is done, then." Alarick grimaced as he sat on his throne. With a small bitter smile, he welcomed the morning sun and its glory.

And turned to ash.

ABOUT THE AUTHOR:

Christopher Watson hales from Las Vegas and currently resides in southern Florida. Favoring fantasy, science fiction, and paranormal occult, he's written over a hundred short stories, a score of novellas, and half a dozen novels.

Forthcoming work:

Science Fiction
From Ashes
Time Loop

Fantasy
Sister Andrew
The Golden-Eyed Girl

ELSEWHERE
E
P
PUBLISHING

THANK YOU FOR READING.

For a complementary electronic version
of this physical work, please go to:
www.elsewherepublishing.com/shop

Load this collection into your cart
and enter the following code:
C0179P89G